...TAE ROSCOMÁIN
...AE ROSCOMÁIN

:e we
rec   !

3

Calling the Wind

Calling the Wind
A Lewis & Clark Story

RITA CLEARY

SAGEBRUSH
Large Print Westerns

Copyright © Rita Cleary, 2005

First published in Great Britain by ISIS Publishing Ltd.
First published in the United States by Five Star

Published in Large Print 2009 by ISIS Publishing Ltd.,
7 Centremead, Osney Mead, Oxford OX2 0ES
United Kingdom
by arrangement with
Golden West Literary Agency

British Library Cataloguing in Publication Data
Cleary, Rita, 1941–
    Calling the wind [text (large print)].
    1. Lewis, Meriwether, 1774–1809 - - Fiction.
    2. Clark, William, 1770–1838 - - Fiction.
    3. Lewis and Clark Expedition (1804–1806) - -
    Fiction.
    4. Explorers - - Pacific Coast (U. S.) - - Fiction.
    5. Historical fiction.
    6. Large type books.
    I. Title
    813.5'4–dc22

ISBN 978–0–7531–8256–7 (hb)

Printed and bound in Great Britain by
T. J. International Ltd., Padstow, Cornwall

Introduction

Calling the Wind is the third of a series about the enlisted men of the Lewis and Clark Expedition of 1804–1806. It continues the stories of John Collins, his friends and fellow members of the Corps of Discovery. They are healthy young men, chosen for their physical strength and abilities. In the society of the day, they are far removed from the illustrious captains. Most were illiterate. Some were craftsmen. At least one, Hugh McNeal, probably enlisted under a false name. One was a slave. Some were part Indian. All knew how to hunt, shoot, and paddle a canoe. Except for the paid scouts, all had enlisted in the United States Army.

Captains Meriwether Lewis and William Clark recorded the native species, geography, and native inhabitants of the unexplored territory but not the experiences of the individual men. In the early 19th Century, writers did not describe emotions or feelings. So Lewis and Clark gave few details of the lives these men lived on the treacherous trek west, and mentioned their names only in passing. You might call them the forgotten men of the expedition.

This story like its predecessors, *River Walk* and *Charbonneau's Gold*, is fictional but most of the characters and many of the circumstances are real. They involve the emotions and ambitions of the many brave men without whose efforts the expedition would not have succeeded. In *Calling the Wind*, they have spent a long, wet winter on the Pacific Coast and are eager to start for home. They must return upriver on the mighty Columbia, over the huge mountain ranges that nearly killed them on the outbound journey. Outbound they did not know the hazards they faced. Homeward bound, they were very aware of the dangers. The British presence on the northwest coast of North America was real. They knew that Alexander MacKenzie had followed the Frazier River across Canada from Hudson's Bay to the Pacific in 1793. And they had heard accounts of Blackfoot brutality from many of the tribes they encountered. They had been honed by the exigencies of wilderness traveling, had listened to Indian accounts, formed their own opinions, and did not always agree with the dictates of their officers. Cultural conflicts arose not only in the face of the native populations, but also within the Corps of Discovery itself. Some men adapt more readily to Indian ways. Some are stoic in the face of sickness and hardship, and some more sympathetic. Some consider the slave a full, responsible member of the troop, and some ignore and reject him. What must have been each man's expectations, fears, and longings? *Calling the Wind* imagines some of the possibilities. And so the saga continues.

CHAPTER
ONE

The tidal surge struck the naked beach with all the weight of the vast Pacific. It was weeks past the winter solstice, when winds and storms are fiercest and the water most violent and cold. A tremolo held, then released, echoed on the battering wind.

William Bratton was down. The ocean had sucked him into its roiling vortex as another mountain of water rolled toward him. John Collins looked up and spotted the flailing arms above the water. The second wave crashed in a tumble of foam, then subsided in deceptive calm. Collins hardly heard the scream over the roar of surf. Bratton's head appeared, farther now from the sanctuary of beach.

Collins pitched his bucket aside and dove into the surf. He was an excellent swimmer, handsome and brave, with broad shoulders made massive by the incessant labor of rowing on the journey with Captains Lewis and Clark. The prodigious effort had produced hard muscles and steely confidence in the young man.

William Bratton was stronger, with the massive build of a man who wields hammer and anvil, but overly confident of his superior strength and a poor swimmer.

He was also older, married, and a reliable counselor and friend.

Collins reached the drowning man in a few powerful strokes, shoved an elbow under his chin, and dove beneath the next crested wave for the beach. Kicking and splashing between the watery swells, he pulled Bratton frantically to the shallows where he gained his footing, gulped air, and blared in Bratton's ear. "Stand, man. Help me."

Sheer terror had convulsed Bratton's craggy face as Collins wiped the weed from his nose. His eyes stared like brown moons. He vomited salt water through his soggy beard and his fingers groped desperately at the shirt on Collins's back. Bratton made no effort to stand and Collins hauled him by the collar beyond the water's edge and released him in a hump on his belly in the sand.

Exhausted, Collins fell to his own hands and knees beside the half-drowned man and rolled onto his back. He coughed before he spoke. "Big man like you, Bratt, should learn to swim." The words, blown with an outrush of air, rang with rebuke.

Bratton shivered and clawed the damp sand with his fingers until the fingernails cracked. Collins watched passively. Stoic endurance was the way of the expedition of Captains Lewis and Clark, of Sergeants Pryor, Ordway, and Gass, of the scout, Drouillard, and all the rest. Bratton wouldn't have wanted sympathy or admitted weakness. But the sight of the burly blacksmith, wet and weak, flat on his belly on the scratchy sand, head turned to the side for breath, face white with fear, hands still crimped and blue with cold, worried Collins. He thought of his own pain, like a scar healed over only on the surface, a wound open and festering beneath. He concealed his special ache, the longing he felt for a Mandan woman named Laughing Water. He would never admit to his longing in front of the lusty, irreverent men of the expedition. They would think him weak.

Collins grumbled testily: "Stay away from the deep if you can't swim. Fill your bucket inshore before the sea floor falls off." Collins himself, while filling his bucket, had slipped off the underwater ledge where the continental shelf suddenly gave way to the deep Pacific. Water from the depths was cleaner, freer of sand and weed, and boiled away to clear, crystal salt that could be traded for food and shelter. But the pull of riptide and sweep of current in the powerful deep could be deadly. Only a strong swimmer like Collins could brace it. Bratton should have known better.

Bratton was not a regular salt-maker. He had arrived as a temporary replacement, so John Colter could go hunting, and he loathed hauling sea water to the giant cauldrons, stoking the ovens, skimming off the weed, and sifting out the sand to extract the precious salt. He was a blacksmith, not a water hauler, and proud of his muscular physique and ability to bend iron and mend the guns and kettles. But every man assigned to the cold and watery effort shouldered his share and counted the hours until the cold, wet labor would end and replacements would snake down to the beach on the switchback trail carved into the cliff at their backs.

It led back up the headland to Fort Clatsop in the sheltered cove on the Netul River, and the warm fellowship of the Corps of Discovery. Named for the local Indian tribe, Fort Clatsop was the expedition's winter quarters.

Collins moved toward the ovens where George Gibson was pulling the remnant of a torn sail that he'd trapped with the water out of his bucket. Gibson shouted into the blow: "Canvas! It'll stop the wind if we can anchor it!" The February wind blew unimpeded from the far side of the Pacific in bursts of watery rage, fierce as the prairie winds of the winter past that packed the snow deeply against the stockade of Fort Mandan.

Collins remembered Fort Mandan well. It lay comfortably tucked by the river one mile from Matootonha village of the Mandan nation. There, he'd met and married Laughing Water. Its round native lodges crowded together for warmth and diverted the bitter north wind that howled endlessly over the plains.

Now he watched the wind seize the smoke from the ovens and dash it brutally against the ragged cliffs of the headland and thought how his own love had shattered like glass against alien customs and culture. If he lived long enough, he hoped, somehow, he could piece together the shards.

Bratton coughed and interrupted his thoughts. George Gibson trudged up to roll him over, and Collins shouted: "Up, Bratt, come to the ovens! Dry out an' get warm!" He moved closer to the gaping fires to warm his own shaking body and help Gibson anchor stakes and stretch the scrap of sail between. It flapped and waved in the incessant wind.

Gibson looked back at Bratton who hadn't moved. "Have to carry him, Johnny."

"He's got arms an' legs. He can walk." Together they attached the unruly canvas, then walked back to Bratton. "You had your rest, Bratt. Want the tide to wash you out again?"

Bratton's answer shrieked like a madman's: "Devils grabbed me, like Cruzatte says they want my guilty soul, pulled me under almost all the way to hell! Damn near killed me!" Old one-eyed Pierre Cruzatte had saved the expedition more than once from a watery maëlstrom, but Cruzatte was a moralist and prophet of doom. Bratton added: "I'm not foolin', Johnny, Gib, I can't move."

"You're talkin'. Your mouth is movin'."

"It's my legs don't go . . . an' that's the truth."

Gibson shook his head and grumbled: "Have to carry him like a sack o' salt, Johnny."

Collins shrugged and muttered: "Grab his bucket before the tide washes it out." Loss of metal objects was a punishable offense. They could not be replaced except with Indian baskets.

Gibson ran to retrieve the bucket, filled it, and returned to the ovens. He walked back up the beach, picked out the clams, then emptied it into a cauldron. He looked at the clams and cast a scornful glance toward the milk-white face of William Bratton. "Dinner, Bratt. Shellfish to fill your bowl." The remark was meant to provoke, but William Bratton hated the slimy, rubbery meat that Gibson and Collins ate raw.

Collins marched back to join Gibson, slapping his sides to get warm. "He gets cold enough, he'll get up. How much wood we got?"

"Enough." Gibson pointed to a giant spruce trunk. "That one rolled down last night. Potts is choppin' more high up the headland." Together they set to work with broad-axe and saw.

Bratton still lay where Collins had left him. "He ain't movin', Gib." Finally Collins trudged back and reached out a hand. "Have a lift, Bratt."

Bratton took the hand but could not propel himself upward.

Collins lips curled in a cynical smile. He called: "Need your help, Gib!"

But Gibson was digging like a rodent in the sand. "Look here, Johnny. See what I found winkin' at me. A flask, shiny an' silver."

Collins looked. "What good it'll do you? Whiskey ran out last summer."

But Gibson tucked the sand-filled flask under his shirt and mumbled: "It holds water better than an Injun mat. It'll hold beer."

Collins laughed. Water had seeped into a canoe and fermented a bale of Indian cous, a potato-like root that the natives ate. Labiche had tasted the stinking mash and pronounced it beer. Gibson drank it and liked it, but it disgusted Collins.

Together they hooked their arms beneath Bratton's armpits and heaved. The big man's legs contracted at

8

the hips and knees. "Stretch 'em straight, Bratt, or walk like a crab." The exhortation did no good. Tears were streaming down the smithy's ruddy cheeks as he turned his face away and his voice cracked like splitting wood: "I can't. God knows I'm tryin'."

Collins exhorted a second time: "Push 'em down, lay 'em flat, man." Bratton only shook his head and let his legs flop. Collins turned to Gibson. "We feed an' warm 'im, he'll feel better. Gass is bringin' fresh meat. He's at the head of the trail now. Got another man with 'im." Patrick Gass, sergeant in charge of the salt-makers, was packing in the meat of two elk that John Colter had killed the day before.

They carried Bratton back to the fires, wrapped him in a blanket, and went back to work. Over the crunch of the axe, Gibson yelled: "He's fakin', Johnny! Got a gal in the Indian village. He wants to get back to Clatsop."

"Woman don' want a man can't walk." Collins knew. He'd been the object of many a woman's dying love even after he married the beautiful Mandan, Laughing Water. He suffered from a glut, never a dearth of prospective mates. But Laughing Water had sent him away for a breech of Indian custom that he hadn't begun to understand. He'd stuffed the memory into a dark recess of his soul and protected it from lusty gossip, but he missed her terribly.

Patrick Gass arrived on the beach with François Labiche. The two men pulled a heavily loaded travois that cut deep furrows in the sand. They dropped it with a thud next to the fire. When he saw Bratton, Gass didn't mince words: "Settin' on your duffs like a fornicating woman or me blind grandmudder knitting, Private Bratton? Stand tall like a proper fighting man." Gass was Irish in his accent and salty in his prose.

Collins explained blandly: "Says he can't walk, sir."

Gass glared like god in judgment at the motionless man. "Can ye pee and shit or must we beseech the saints in heaven to raise you up, Private Bratton?"

A blush of anger suddenly banished the fear in Bratton's white face. He grit his teeth. With his arms, he pushed his knees under him, writhed like a worm, and fell back.

Labiche, a former sailor and pirate who had witnessed accidents on sailing ships, pulled Bratton's leggings above his ankle and pricked the skin with the point of his knife. Blood flowed, but Bratton didn't flinch, and Labiche declared: "He's telling the truth. He has no feeling and no movement in his legs."

Silence fell as the four men digested the awful truth and weighed the consequences. Gass narrowed his eyes and drew in his lips. "If he's not better by morning, I'll beg the cap'n to send a replacement." His tone softened when he muttered: "How much salt you good lads 'ave?"

Collins replied: "Two bushels. Not enough."

"I'll carry what you 'ave back to Clatsop."

Collins cooked a hearty stew of shellfish and roots, but what should have been a welcome visit was gloomy and silent. Bratton hardly ate. The other men circled around him in the fire's orange glow behind the ragged windbreak, as gray clouds gave way to black of night. Sporadically the gusty wind blew smoke over the men.

10

Bratton moaned and Collins mumbled; "Breathe it in, Bratt. Indians say smoke cleanses. Burn out your devils. Burn out the sickness that ails you."

When finally they rolled themselves in their bedding, Bratton began to whimper like a beaten cur. The moaning wind echoed the desperation of a dying man. Collins caught a word here, a sentence there, as Bratton's voice floated on the wind. "How am I gonna ford a river, climb a mountain? How am I gonna get home? Can't stand to shoot. Can't kneel to row. Can't swing an axe." He ranted on.

"Maybe you won't have to, Bratt," Collins whispered below the level of hearing as he lay awake and waited for Bratton to sleep. When Bratton's litany didn't stop, he moved his bed nearer François Labiche who'd shared his canoe since the previous April. Labiche would know how to silence Bratton. No matter what the hardships they'd faced, Labiche, ugly, wiry, battle-scarred pirate and gambler, always found a way to ease the burden. Labiche fostered every man's hope.

Labiche was awake, and he spoke to Collins. "We carried Whitehouse, Johnny, when the canoe ran him over. We'll carry Bratton all the way back to Saint Louie if we have to, load him in a boat or on a horse with the rest of the baggage. Been lucky. Only lost one man so far."

"Horses're a whole month's march away, pirate, at the base of the mountains, with the Nez Percé, two hundred miles of rock an' rapid." Collins rolled over, closed his eyes, and burrowed into the sand to escape the howling wind that hurled the roaring ocean into the slab rocks of the headland and sucked the sand from their quiet cove.

Next morning Bratton was no better. The day was gray, hemmed on all sides with colorless mist. Gass and Labiche left with a bushel of salt each, and John Potts arrived with a travois of wood that he stacked near the ovens. Collins and Gibson continued the drudgery, filling buckets, stoking the fires, and slogging through ankle-deep sand the hundred weary paces from the edge of the lapping waves to the boiling pots. Smudges of damp, black smoke snaked skyward from flaming ovens.

In the afternoon, Billy Warner and Joe Fields arrived with orders from the captains. "Collins returns with Bratton. We come to replace the two o' you."

"Bratton can't walk."

"Cap'n says carry him. Load him on Potts's travois."

Collins groaned because Potts had returned to the headland and he would have to haul Bratton up the high cliff to where Potts worked.

Gibson summed it up: "Want him to fly like a bird? You'll ache, Johnny, but you're leavin' this cursed beach, movin' closer to your Mandan lady, an' movin' to dry, hard land that doesn't sink every time you set your foot down, like this seamy, wet sand."

When morning came, the stiff west wind drove the water farther up the beach. Gibson, Warner, and Joe Fields had set to hauling water early before the tide ran out and lengthened the distance they had to walk back to the ovens. Collins loaded Bratton over his shoulder and started up the trail to the headland. At the top, he found the travois and he stopped to rest. Potts was out somewhere cutting wood. Collins resented a man who feigned work, refused to shoulder his share, and let others take up the slack, but that wasn't William Bratton. There'd been a few such men, early in the journey, on the way out. The sergeants, captains, and Georges Drouillard had exposed the culprits but not before Charles Floyd had died trying to compensate for Moses Reed. Would Floyd have survived if he'd hadn't worked so hard? Collins thought so. And now Bratton, hard-working until now, would not perform his share. Hardship changed a man, made some better, some worse. Collins turned his face to the wind and looked down at the men, crawling like ants over the sand to the ovens, and wondered how the tough labor had affected Bratton. Finally he turned blade-thin eyes on the paralyzed man. "You're not foolin' us, are you, Bratt?"

Bratton averted his gaze. "Can't blame you for thinkin' it. Wouldn't blame you fer leavin' me here."

A shadow passed over Collins's brow as he admitted in his heart that he was tempted. He answered truthfully: "Captains would never allow it, Bratt."

"But you would. I'm no more use than a lame horse or a broken wheel. Shove me over the cliff. Let the sharks an' the deep put an end to me." The comment pricked like sharp, cold flint.

Collins inhaled and answered: "We didn't leave Charlie Floyd even though he was dyin'." He bit back his lips. "No sharks here. Water's too cold. Captain Lewis'll do for you at Clatsop. He's an educated man, knows his cures."

"Gimme Rush's thunder pills, same's he done Floyd . . . an' Floyd's dead." Bratton remembered vividly the painful death. He kept talking as if speech could release the terrible fear that filled his consciousness. "Floyd died o' colic. No cure for colic, man or horse. Colicky horse knows when to lay down an' die and an honest man knows when to put a wobbly horse outta his misery. No cure for me sure's I can't lift a leg an' pee like a mongrel dog. I'm done an' I know it."

Collins felt his throat constrict. "Like it or not, you're alive, Bratt, talkin', breathin' an' I won't put a knife to your throat or let you die." But he'd seen colicky horses writhe in pain and die a gruesome death. He wouldn't wish that on any man.

Bratton had seen them, too. "It ain't the pain. Feel like I'm dead already. Feel nothin'."

Collins sucked back his breath. At least a horse would cow-kick and snort and lunge until the pain consumed him. Floyd had worked until the sweat poured from his feverish skin and dust and vomit spattered his golden beard. His death was ugly, smelly, dirty. Maybe a shot to the head or a knife to the throat like they gave a horse would have been merciful. Bloody business, killing a horse, but Floyd's death was longer, more painful. Collins cringed when he thought of Floyd. He'd helped dig Floyd's grave. Now he blurted angrily at Bratton: "You're a man, not a horse. Man-killin's work for God or the devil, not me."

"Injuns leave their old ones behind all the time. Out here, across those mountains, one good horse is worth a hundred of me."

14

Collins didn't answer. Rudely he picked up the travois and dragged it away inland. He threaded his way over rocks and between trunks of massive redwood and Sitka spruce. The travois jigged and rocked and Bratton cried out: "You want me to suffer so's you can act the hero, so's the captain'll smother you with praise, thank you for savin' my life!"

Collins dropped the travois with a crash, stepped back, and beat down the impulse to drive a fist into Bratton's mouth. "Maybe I'm savin' you for death, Bratt, but I'm not listenin' to you. I hope you go straight to hell." He picked moss from the crevices of an ancient tree, rolled it into balls, and stuffed them into his ears. Silently he resumed the march the eight long miles to Fort Clatsop while Bratton lay, morose and silent, as the grave.

They arrived at the fort in the late afternoon and Collins reported to Meriwether Lewis. His words were flat, without sympathy. "Surf hit him. Says he can't walk, sir."

Lewis called for his lancet and fleam, and bled Bratton on the spot. He assigned York, Clark's slave, to watch the sick man. In the days that followed, Bratton weakened more. His arms flopped listlessly. He could not grip a spoon or lift food to his mouth. Lewis tried every remedy he knew: some the Indian woman prepared, some Dr. Benjamin Rush of Philadelphia, the most respected physician of the day, prescribed, and some gleaned from tribal shamans. Still William Bratton languished.

Old Cruzatte pronounced harsh judgment: "Almighty God has called the curse of Satan down upon him, no less a curse than the mark of Cain."

York heard Cruzatte's verdict and a twinge of protest crossed his stoic brow. But Bratton also heard and railed against the black man: "Contaminate my feed with Cain's guilty paws." He spit out the food that York spooned into his mouth, and Lewis's dog lapped up the morsels. Finally Lewis ordered Collins to cook and serve.

Weeks passed. York cleaned his bedding, washed, and carried Bratton. Collins and Labiche spooned in his dinner. Bratton complained endlessly of the damp, of the rain, of the cold or the smoke in his quarters, and of the tainted care of the black man. "Blacks is worse than reds. Injuns'll fight you, but the blackies'll poison you." He even blasted Labiche who fed him: "Filthy pirate you are, skin baked black in the sun, nose skewered like a piece o' meat to yer face . . . you look more like an Injun than Charbonneau's woman."

Labiche dropped the spoon. Charbonneau's woman was Shoshone, a mother and a valuable and respected member of the group. He fired back: "On a ship, we'd chain you in the hold for that, throw you slops from the galley, let you slurp it like a dog, an', when you died, we'd launch your stinking body into the sea, no grave, no marker, a sack for a coffin, if you're lucky, and cold blue water for your grave."

"I'm not afraid to die."

"No, Bratt, you're afraid to live." Labiche licked the spoon, filled it, and held it to Bratton's mouth.

16

Bratton clamped his teeth and twisted his head away. "I ain't eatin' your spit."

Labiche laughed and snapped at Collins: "Call the sergeant."

Sergeant Nathaniel Pryor came and thundered: "Eat, Private Bratton. That's an order." When Bratton still refused, Pryor's patience cracked: "Hold him, Collins. Pirate, force his mouth open." Collins pinned his shoulders while Labiche squeezed open his jaw and Pryor jammed the spoon between his teeth. "Now clamp his mouth shut until he swallows." He handed the spoon back to Labiche.

The scene repeated itself daily, but Bratton's muscled body tensed and thinned. Collins never returned to the beach. March blew in with a lion wind as the quantities of salt increased. Finally, on March 22nd at morning muster, Captain Lewis announced: "Tomorrow, soldiers, we leave this swamp."

John Colter, standing at attention next to Collins breathed: "At long last."

Collins cheered until Sergeant Pryor fingered him: "Collins, get Bratt. Feed and water him good, an' tell York to lash him in your boat."

When he went for Bratton, the sick man mocked him rudely: "Struttin' back to that woman, eh, Johnny? Least you're goin' whole."

Collins didn't answer.

CHAPTER
TWO

Captain Richard Markham of the good ship *Phoenix* stepped to the center of the quarterdeck and commanded: "Weigh anchor, Mister Eagleton."

"Weigh anchor!" Eagleton repeated the order with a shrill squawk. It carried across the decks to every able seaman, and they started to reel in the heavy anchor chain and climb the rigging to unfurl the sails.

Markham was glad as the next man to be leaving this hellhole of islands, shoals, capricious winds, conflicting currents, and leeward shores. He smiled and headed to the wardroom to record the date in the ship's log, December 2, 1805.

The HMS *Phoenix*, with eighteen guns and a letter of marque from the British crown, was one year and five months out of Liverpool. A sturdy, triple-masted sloop, she had braved the southern seas, rounded Cape Horn, and entered the vast Pacific last May, just ahead of the southern winter.

The Pacific was a Spanish lake. The danger of seizure by Spanish pirates increased as the *Phoenix* sailed north. She had touched a lonely island briefly for fresh water, greens, and quinoa, and stopped for refitting at Lahaina in the Sandwich Islands. In the fall of the year, she sailed east on a reconnaissance mission to the American coast. But hammering winds drove her south toward Mexico before she turned north past the perilous shores of California. That was where the fever struck. *Gaol fever* they called it in the London prisons, but it was prevalent on the ships, too, and especially virulent in the crowded, damp quarters below deck where the able seamen hung their hammocks. The sickness doubled a man over in pain, so that he could no longer climb a rig or hoist a sail. Captain Markham and the officers' mess remained untouched. They paid no attention and sailed on.

When the ship's carpenter, a cranky Scotsman named Parrish, heaved his dinner over the gunwales into the sea, replacement spars were running low and Lieutenant Eagleton mentioned it to the captain. "Fresh water, sir, is nearly gone and Parrish is sick, sir, as are others. Prudence dictates a landing to allow them to recuperate."

Markham nodded, but the leeward wind was dangerously strong and the coast rocky. "No landing here. Only shifting shoals and craggy bluffs and Spanish gun ships on patrol. The Columbia straits are a safer haven." He looked at his charts. "They are not far." He lied.

A powerful westerly blew in frequent cold rain and the crew set out cups and buckets as fresh water fell like manna from heaven. It stagnated in the scuppers and smelled like bilge swill and there was never enough. A landing, no matter how risky, was ever more urgent.

Still Markham had pressed on past the coast of Spanish California.

The *Phoenix* was a British merchantman seeking furs, but Markham had a more pressing mission. The British Admiralty needed to know the extent and strength of the Spanish presence on the western shores of North America. England had declared war with Napoléonic France whose expanding empire had conquered Spain. Merchant ships in the service of Britain had disappeared on the distant shores of the Spanish colonies. Blame centered on Spain's new ruler, Joseph, brother of the hated Napoléon Bonaparte, and England's bitter enemy. The Spanish governor at Monterrey had a greedy eye for enemy cargo and seized any strange ship that sailed too close to California's coast. Markham's good friend, Captain Joshua Hale, and his crew of fifty hardy seamen languished in a California jail, so the story went, if he was still alive. No one had heard a word of him for over two years.

Markham mused to himself: "Cowardly man, Hale, to allow his ship to be taken without a fight." He sat nightly under the low ceiling of the wardroom at a wide mahogany table studying his charts, assured that such a fate would never befall the *Phoenix*. A lantern glowed and swayed with the gentle motion of the ship and spattered uneven light on the open chart. It was December 12th and Markham pricked the chart with a sharp fingernail. The *Phoenix* lay at exactly thirty-eight degrees north last noon when the sun broke through the clouds enough to take accurate bearings. He moved his finger along the wall of coastline to a point east and

20

muttered: "Here is a safe harbor north of the Spanish settlements. Nootka Sound is too far." He pointed at the estuary of the Columbia River.

Only his orderly was present to hear the comment. "Shall I tell the lieutenant, sir?"

"Yes do, Mister Cawley. And tell him to bring Mister Ochoa. Ochoa has sailed these shores before. And bring rum." Ochoa was the half-Carib Indian, dark-skinned ship's cook. The other half of his lineage was also doubtful. His skin was the color of weak tea.

Cawley held the door wide as Eagleton and Ochoa entered Markham's presence. Eagleton seated himself comfortably in a high-backed chair. Ochoa waited for the captain to direct him to a stool. Markham poured three flagons of rum, sipped his own, and pushed two across the table. "Gentlemen, I want to hear your honest comment . . . no flattery, no evasion, only the stark, undiluted truth."

"Aye, sir." Eagleton grinned broadly and sipped his rum. Ochoa was silent.

Markham kicked his feet up on the table. "We sail north, to a safe harbor beyond the dominions of Spain where there is good water and wood for ship's fittings." He did not add what Parrish, the carpenter, had told him: that the *Phoenix*'s timbers were wormy; that, without refitting, she could not withstand tacking into the fierce Pacific winds; that she could never reach Lahaina again without major repair. Parrish, the captain decided, had exaggerated. He continued casually: "I count on you gentlemen to sustain the co-operation and continued loyalty of the crew."

Mutiny, he knew, was a calculated risk. He ran a finger around the rim of his mug, took a long swallow, and raised his mug high. "A toast, gentlemen, to the glory of Britain and the defeat of the French devil." He leaned back, stroked the soft velvet facings of his coat, and appraised each man with a narrow, calculating eye.

Ochoa was tall for an Indian, about six feet with a beak of nose and perceptive, intelligent eyes, windows to a superior brain. Eagleton was also tall, but fair and blond and his eyes puffed from the ravages of strong drink. Ochoa lowered his gaze, swirled the colorless liquid in his flagon, and barely wet his tongue.

Markham continued, snapping his syllables stiffly like a flag in the wind: "We could sail west to the summer islands but they have their perils. Life is too easy. When last I was in the islands, we lost men . . . deserters." He cast an appraising glance at his captive listeners and added: "I hear there is rich profit to be made on this northerly coast . . . in pelts." He sipped his rum and repeated: "For those who can forego the tropic warmth, great profit lies in wait, in furs." He let the long, sensuous syllable rest like a delicious sweet on his tongue as he repeated: "Furs." He paused, then resumed: "Mister Ochoa, what can you tell us of the inhabitants of these fair shores? What language do they speak, what kind of welcome awaits us, and what opportunities might we expect for profit?"

Ochoa crinkled his bronzed face. He was not used to being consulted by officers on matters of import, but he had visited these shores before. His deep-set black eyes glared over his huge hooked nose. His full lips seemed to pucker and shrink. In barely accented English, he spoke his mind. "They're friendly, sir. They speak a peculiar jargon. Their furs are smoother than your sword's polished blade and softer than the pink backside of a newborn, but they are bloody, cunning thieves." He sniffled and added: "They have only baskets in which to cook their food. They crave our kettles, needles, and fish hooks." He snapped his teeth shut on a gush of air. "And our rum."

Markham let his feet fall with a thud to the floor, sat up, and raised a curious brow. The man spoke well for a half-breed cook. He inquired: "No muskets? Don't all natives want guns?"

"They're river people, traders not warriors, fishermen not hunters, sir. They fish all year. The waters in the bays do not freeze."

A buttery grin spread across Markham's pinched face. "Then kettles and rum they shall have for their precious furs that will buy us Chinese silk and spice and the red poppy's white powder. Only a Spanish galleon is a richer prize." Markham rolled up his charts and rapped them smartly against the table's rim. He'd laid in a good supply of rum at Lahaina, where Ochoa had signed on. Still smiling, he turned to his lieutenant. "You heard, Mister Eagleton. At forty-six degrees north, bear east on an easy reach, downwind. Seek a safe harbor. We'll trade and stay the winter."

Eagleton cast a black glance at Ochoa, and he protested: "'Tis late in the year, sir. Do you take the word of a black man?"

Markham raised a brow and looked down the sharp bridge of his nose. "I have made fair assessment of the season, Lieutenant. Mister Ochoa assures me that ice is not a threat. Perhaps you've spent too much of your life seated on soft cushions in drawing rooms that you cringe at a bite of invigorating cold." His voice sliced like a thin blade, and Eagleton recoiled. Markham explained: "In the spring, we'll sail south again to the fair Sandwich Islands where the fruit is sweet and the fair ladies eager companions to His Majesty's worthy seamen. And the furs in the *Phoenix*'s hold will make us rich."

Ochoa lifted a hesitant hand. "Pardon, sir, something more."

Markham frowned. He didn't welcome interruption from a ship's cook and drummed his fingers irritably on the corner of the chart, but Ochoa insisted: "They pant like wolves on a scent, sir. These natives, they'll steal, sir, whatever is open to view or tips their fancy."

Markham's eyes narrowed. He took another gulp of rum and licked his pink lips. "So we shall use their cupidity to our advantage, spread chum on the waters, Mister Ochoa, and let the greedy sharks bite." With a curl of lip, he met Eagleton's nervous glare and continued: "Allow only foragers to land and confine the remaining crew to the ship for the duration of our stay."

Eagleton quipped — "Aye, aye, sir." — and dropped his gaze.

Markham continued: "Mister Ochoa will keep the sick well plied with quinoa and grog. How many gallons of fresh water have we?"

"Without rain, rationed, we've barely enough, sir, but the rains should come steadily here on the north coast."

"Excellent, Mister Ochoa." Markham's face spread in a self-satisfied grin.

The *Phoenix* dropped anchor in a quiet estuary, and it began to rain. Foragers, under Lieutenant Eagleton, went ashore, bought roots and fresh greens and salmon from friendly Chinook Indians who rowed their canoes out to the ship, clambered up the rope ladders, over the gunwales, and onto the decks. They brought furs and baskets of roots. They left with kettles, beads, knives, barrels of watered rum, and an occasional musket.

Enthroned on his quarterdeck, Markham surveyed his realm. He had secured all hatches and ordered the eviction of any Indian thief who overstepped enforced boundaries. Eager natives often grew unmanageable. One Chinook, caped in fine otter trimmed with white ermine tails, clambered aboard with a retinue of servants and Markham nodded to Eagleton: "The head man, bring him to the wardroom, Lieutenant. And get Mister Ochoa. He knows the language."

"Ochoa, aye, sir." Eagleton spat the name acidly, but he followed the order to the letter.

Markham was seated again comfortably at his table when the head man arrived. He was a square man, clad in only a truss of matted grass pulled between his legs and a luxurious fur cape. The profile of his face slanted in a straight line from the tip of his nose to the peak of his skull. He was darkly complexioned. His brow was broad, his cheek bones high, his eyes spread wide apart. They peered out from his misshapen face over a flattened nose and expanse of clownish lips. He had cut his black bangs in a straight line across his brow and clipped the remaining hair evenly just below the lobe of his ear, so that on three sides it framed his ghoulish face. Markham retreated behind his broad table and directed him to a chair, but the head man ignored the offer and squatted crab-like on his heels.

Ochoa ducked furtively under the doorjamb a few seconds later and stood to one side. The Chinook addressed Ochoa who most nearly resembled him in coloring and alone could make intelligent sense of his jargon.

Markham stared at his manicured fingernails, but he caught several words that parroted English and he came alert with a start at the word, *dolla*. Dollars were American currency. This brute must have heard of dollars, and knew who the Americans were. Did he also know the commercial use of currency? Did he comprehend the value of a dollar and the greater value of the British pound sterling? Markham had an ample supply of pounds sterling that he was saving for use in China. He did not want to waste them on a heathen Chinook.

Gradually the captain let his wishes be known — furs in exchange for rum and kettles, beads, cloth, and needles.

The head man smacked his rubbery lips and cackled: "I give pelts." He stabbed at the English word and let it reverberate, narrowed his eyes, and added: "And *klootchmen*."

"Women, sir." Ochoa understood immediately. "He will give us his women for our rum, guns, kettles, beads, and pretty coats with gold braid."

Markham's impatience bordered on anger, and he blared back: "We want furs, not women, Mister Ochoa. Tell him we want only furs."

The head man pretended surprise and rambled on about the riches other traders had brought. A Captain Davidson had come in a ship with twin masts, twenty-four guns, and crates of kettles and muskets. Jack Skelley, the infamous, one-legged captain of the *Stork*, had brought knives and beads and silver buckles. And then there were strange white men who arrived in canoes and came with the wild, gushing waters of the river and the rising sun out of the eastern mountains. These men, dressed in ragged hides, preferred the sinewy meat of skinny elk to the rich, fat flesh of the salmon. They were disagreeable, insulting guests, with little of value to trade, not like the generous sailors from the ships. And they scorned the advances of his most alluring *klootchmen*.

Alarm flashed in Markham's devious mind. Other whites had arrived by land. Who? Spaniards from California, or possibly Russians from the north — the political import was threatening. He had heard that the Americans had dispatched explorers, but he doubted they could have ventured this far. Still, he questioned Ochoa carefully: "From the east? Surely he means from the north or south."

"He says east, from the rivers, sir." Ochoa pointed and waited before adding: "He called them *Boston men*."

Markham's face reddened as frustration burst: "I heard his infernal chattering, Ochoa." He perceived Americans as rebellious, treasonous, impoverished stepchildren of the British crown. How dare they attempt to invade the lucrative fur trade that the British had established.

Eagleton filled the silence: "There's Welshmen settled America, sir, a thousand years ago, the princely sons of King Madoc."

"Boston was not settled by Welshmen, Mister Eagleton." The captain's fury was mounting.

Eagleton would not be quiet. "They were brave fighters, sir, of a royal house." His voice faltered, cut short by Markham's steely gaze.

Markham waved away the comments: "The invention of your besotted imagination, Mister Eagleton."

Eagleton recoiled at the rebuke while Markham questioned the head man more thoroughly and listened attentively to his jabbering. *Boston men* were Americans. American ships had entered the estuary and Americans had purchased fat dogs, wood, and roots from the natives. The American rascals had spread their perfidy far beyond the borders of their seventeen petty states, far beyond the newly purchased lands of Louisiana, and Captain Richard Markham of the HMS *Phoenix* determined to stop them. But he needed to confirm the reports of this ignorant native, to learn where the traitors camped, and how great a threat they posed. He considered sending Eagleton ashore to reconnoiter. Eagleton, an officer from an old landed family of Wales, had served the Royal Navy since the age of twelve and owed his lieutenancy to social connection and the scarcity of available men during wartime. But Eagleton lacked intelligence, was prone to fits of jealousy, and worked well only when a superior made decisions for him. Invariably Eagleton gambled and arrived back from shore leave drunk and penniless. More than once they had had to carry him back. Besides his fair skin, protruding brow, and crag of nose would stand out like a poppy in a pasture among the short, dark, flat-faced Chinooks.

Markham's icy blue gaze settled on Ochoa. The man was new to the service of Britain. He had a Spanish name but spoke fluent English and harbored a deep-seated hatred of Spain. He never revealed the cause of his hatred to the captain or officers, but the crew had heard the story in the galley and it had seeped through the loose filter of ship's gossip to the officers. Ochoa was dark-skinned, dark enough that a Spanish trader had seized him on the streets of Havana and tried to sell him as a black African slave. He had escaped on a homemade raft and been picked up, half dead, by British pirates off Barbados. A command of English had saved his life and he had recovered quickly. His talents as translator and cook had quickly become apparent to all.

Aboard the *Phoenix*, Ochoa prepared meals. In taste, they were delicious; in quantity, bountiful and more appetizing than the over-boiled mush the official cook prepared. So when the cook was found one morning floating face down in a tropical calm, Ochoa assumed his duties.

29

Now Markham motioned Ochoa to follow him to the quarterdeck. He continued speaking as he walked out the wardroom door. "Crofton will prepare the mess. I need information and you quite possibly are the only one among us who can ferret it out. Have you ever been a spy, Mister Ochoa?" The captain did not turn around but kept walking briskly.

Ochoa, who hurried behind, had learned never to admit inexperience. He uttered a deliberate: "Yes, sir." Then he qualified his statement. "Once, sir, years ago."

Markham clomped across the wooden planks, hands clutched behind his back, then climbed the ladder to the quarterdeck before he turned to face the startled cook. "I intend to sail to Nootka Sound, Mister Ochoa. I have the assurances from Mister MacKenzie's log that it is a safe harbor. But I want you to go ashore here, mingle with the natives, ascertain if in fact Americans are a presence on this coast. Discover how they have come, and how long they intend to stay. For this, I will assign to you the ship's launch for the duration of the winter months, but if you can obtain native transport, so much the better. I will give you a swivel gun, a brace of pistols for your personal protection, powder and ball, an officer's dress uniform and bicorne hat, trade goods enough to impress the natives, and three of my best men. Know that by this act, you will help defeat the despotic rule of our mutual enemy, Spain, and her tempestuous king, Joseph Bonaparte. And you will waylay the rebel Americans." He hesitated and cast a knife-like glance directly into Ochoa's fierce black eyes.

"Perform well, Mister Ochoa, and I will double your pay."

Ochoa sensed his growing prestige. He bowed and barely smiled. "I will do my utmost, sir," but his true thoughts remained confined in the backwaters of his brain where a persistent question nagged: *How do I know you will not abandon me?*

Markham was smiling now, elated by his own apparent brilliance. "The information you will have gained, Mister Ochoa, will advance the glory of Britain and insure my own and your prompt promotion."

Ochoa let his own lips spread in a pasty grin. The width of his mouth accentuated the broad Indian features of his face. The captain laid a persuasive hand on his shoulder. "What say you, sir? Do you accept?" Markham did not offer his hand.

Ochoa did not hesitate. "Aye, sir, with pleasure."

They loaded the launch with kettles, beads, crates of muskets, lead and canisters of black powder, and casks of watered rum. Markham dressed Ochoa handsomely in his own dress coat with gold-braided epaulets at the shoulders and placed a bicorne hat upon his head so that the dark man resembled an exotic prince when he and three aides stepped into the launch for the trip ashore. The natives conducted them with highest honor to their village, ushered them to their own spacious lodge, and regaled them with gifts of silken furs, feasting, and beautiful *klootchmen*.

In a few days, Ochoa had confirmed the American presence and sent a messenger to the *Phoenix*. The messenger returned promptly with a written dispatch from the captain that read: See that the Americans receive no help from the Chinook and if in any way you can make their presence unpalatable, proceed with my blessing and the blessing of His Majesty the King. Ten golden guineas accompanied the dispatch.

Ochoa settled in for a comfortable duration. One month passed before he sent another message and received a second dispatch from his captain. He unrolled the sealed scroll. It read: On receipt of this dispatch, send word east if possible to the Blackfeet tribe and Mr. Larkin, the British factor there. Tell them the Boston men will snatch away lands and rivers and curtail the flow of trade goods from Mother England. Tell all the tribes loyal to England that the Americans will supply guns to their enemies and cause their dominions to shrink. Ten more guineas accompanied the dispatch.

Ochoa's eyes crinkled with mirth as he read it. He repeated aloud: "Send word east, inland, over mountains?" He laughed and mused. "I should get lost first." Ochoa squeezed the parchment until it crinkled, tossed it to the ground, and concluded that the captain was washing his hands of him and departing for warmer climes.

Ochoa was living better than he ever had in his life. He had a warm lodge, bountiful meals, and women at his beck and call. He had Markham's golden guineas, a swivel gun, brace of pistols, sword, and a pirate's affection for weapons and gold. No more smelly, cramped hammock in the damp belly of a ship; living here among the natives, he was safe from seizure by slavers and esteemed and honored by the native population. If the *Phoenix* never returned, if Captain Markham died of the scurvy, or if the entire British navy sank, he didn't care.

CHAPTER
THREE

Dawn broke early over the high stockade of Fort Clatsop on Sunday, March 23, 1806. John Collins rolled out of his bedding and glared out the door of the hut. It was raining lightly — it was always raining. Collins could count the sunny days at Fort Clatsop on the fingers of his hands — six days of sunlight in three long, rain-soaked months. The hot prairie sun was as distant a memory as was the satin sheen of ice on the river.

Gray mist filtered through the doorway and hovered over the lumpy forms of Whitehouse, Labiche, and Shannon who still slept. Collins nudged them awake and pulled on his shirt before rolling his bedding into a tight ball.

From a dark corner of the hut, a voice sounded. "Cold in here."

"You awake, Bratt?"

"Never slept all night. Brain's still alive an' thinkin'."

Collins clenched his fists, thrust them tightly against his thighs, and let words alone pour out his anger: "You want to suffer, don't you, Bratt? You like makin' us squirm an' sweat an' wait on your every whim like slaves to your lord almighty."

The fire crackled and sent a shower of sparks up the chimney. Bratton didn't answer. The long winter's struggle, the rain, the mud, the wind that blew wet salt in his face, and now his debilitating paralysis had hammered the man down. Bratton closed his eyes.

Collins raised his hand, ready to strike. "Answer me. Look at me, you ungrateful shirker."

Labiche stayed Collins's arm. "Don't hurt him more."

Collins's resentment flared. "He uses his weakness to needle and jibe. It was me carried him home."

Labiche replied: "Aye, he knows, an' now he'll be ridin' in our boat." Slowly he released Collins's arm. "So will the slave." He paused, then added: "Come help load the salt."

It began to rain as they walked to the shoreline where the bushels of salt were stacked. Labiche began heaving bushels, relaying them to Collins, who placed them in the boat. York laid Bratton lengthwise, propped him against the sacks of salt, and tucked an elk-skin around him to keep him dry. With thongs of tough bark, Labiche bound him tightly into the boat. Finally the black man walked to the edge of the forest, fell to his knees, and raised his arms to the watery sky.

Collins heaved another bushel of salt and muttered: "What for's he prayin'? Should be helpin' . . . loadin' the salt."

Labiche shook his head: "Captain gives him woman's work, nursin' the sick. You an' I wouldn't do it. Wouldn't want to. He's prayin' for Bratton to get his wobbly legs strong so he doesn't have to carry him an' we don't have to paddle his dead weight like sacks of salt upriver. The slave knows. Bratton's lost a slice of freedom. When York prays, he's prayin' for Bratt and himself, prayin' his strength won't wither before the captain sets him free. And he endures Bratt's complaints better than you, Johnny. Never raised a finger in anger."

Collins had to admit that York performed flawlessly, silently, patiently. As Bratton worsened, washing, dressing, feeding, toileting, all York's minor labors multiplied.

The rain stopped, the sun poked through the clouds, and Labiche passed the last bushel to Collins. "Pack it high and dry, Johnny." He fell back on his buttocks on the gravelly beach. Then by way of conversation, he added: "Think Fort Mandan's still standin'? Think your woman's waitin'?"

The question, in front of Bratton, made Collins blush, then bristle. He'd suffered in silence, tried hard to contain the memories, but he couldn't stop curious speculation. He still loved Laughing Water and thought of her frequently. He sat back beside Labiche, stretched out his long legs, and tried to sound dismissive. "Probably married her off to the next available brave . . . whoever paid the price. Her grandmother set the hounds on me."

Labiche knew the whole lurid story and was not fooled. He'd won the horses that bought Laughing Water for lovesick Collins and the two had been fast friends ever since, but they made an unlikely pair. Labiche, short, wiry, part Indian, part Creole from the

Mississippi Delta, had been a seaman and pirate. He could wield a knife and sword better than any man in the corps, but the scars of battle had so disfigured his face that women found him ghoulish. He took his pleasure in his collection of razor-sharp blades and vicariously in the romantic conquests of the handsome and magnetic Collins.

Tall, with the long, hard muscles of his Irish ancestry, Collins came from the wooded interior of the Maryland hills. He was a herdsman and woodsman. With dark blue eyes, regular features, and a shock of thick blond hair that he cut with a knife when it fell in his eyes, he could swim, paddle a boat, and shoot with precision. But he had an Irishman's temper and strong independent spirit. Drouillard, the expedition's best scout, had recruited Collins and defended him early in the trip after the headstrong young Collins broke strict Army discipline in a bout of drunkenness. Drouillard had taught him patience and perseverance. The self-control so necessary on the long trek with the salty men of the corps was a harder lesson.

Labiche nodded and grinned: "The old crone's probably dead, Johnny, hounds, too."

"Or waitin' with a war club to crack my skull." Collins closed his eyes. The memory was still raw.

"You could stay with the Mandans, make your life with Laughing Water." Labiche flipped the remark like a wild card into the conversation. An angry glance from Collins diverted him. "Me, I'll take my pay in land on a clear creek in Missouri, maybe find a woman who'll love me for my heart and not my face."

"She'll love you for your quick eye and nimble fingers and the winnings that'll make her rich." Collins laughed lightly.

But Labiche was serious: "I can raise cows. No animal ever shied from an ugly face." He smiled and his crooked face looked almost friendly. "I farmed before I sailed. Never told you that. Cotton, in the delta, blistering hot, the delta." He put a hand to his cheek and grimaced. "Some men here have women back home . . . Shields, Bratton, Captain Clark."

He looked up. York had returned with a *pacquet* of meat and a skin of water and tucked it beside Bratton for the trip. Labiche continued as if the black man were absent or deaf: "Blackie probably has his blackie woman and a passel of blackie chicks. Valuable property, blackie chicks. Bet he makes chicks faster than Clark can sell 'em."

"Not makin' chicks out here," Collins said.

York's eyes flared suddenly. Then he dropped them and turned away, and Labiche rattled on. "Yes, he is. Indian girls think he's a great warrior." Labiche paused and grew pensive. "Only one woman I ever loved who loved me back. Died giving birth. Life flows like the rivers, blows by like the wind, too fast. It can pass a man by, suck him down, blow him away. But land underfoot is permanent." He heaved the last bushel at Collins who lowered it into the boat.

The call to muster sounded. Labiche and Collins collected their meager gear and shuffled into Fort Clatsop's yard for the last call of the roll. As Collins took his place, alphabetically, in front of Colter, behind

38

the space where Bratton should have stood, gray clouds opened and rain poured down again. The corps saluted the Stars and Stripes and presented arms, but sight of the wet, sagging flag unsettled John Collins. He was glad to be leaving the damp and the rot, but what awaited him on the way home saddened him. His white family's home was a crowded log cabin in Frederick, Maryland — mother, father, fourteen children. A grown son had to leave, find his own way. Collins's Indian home was a comfortable earth lodge at Matootonha, the largest Mandan trading village, where Laughing Water and her family resided. But because he refused to share her with a decrepit old warrior during what he perceived as a frenzied fertility rite, the family matriarch had castigated Laughing Water and thrown him out. What awaited him on his return, he did not know, and he suffered in silence.

Now he braced his shoulders smartly as William Clark reviewed the ranks and Meriwether Lewis, thin, pale, in pieces of his old dress uniform, trying to maintain the dignity of his rank, lowered the ragged, water-soaked flag. It descended slowly, like the unraveling of Collins's own life, and he wondered where next they would raise the flag, if he would live to see it whip in the prairie wind over Fort Mandan or wave on the bluff over the muddy Mississippi at St. Louis.

"All accounted for, sirs, except Drouillard. He hasn't yet come in." The statement in Sergeant Gass's melodious brogue made Collins wince. Where was Drouillard? Surely they wouldn't leave without

Drouillard. He watched in silence as the sergeants carefully folded the flag and presented it to Lewis who tucked it reverently under his arm.

No one moved as Lewis scanned the high, moss-encrusted stockade of the fort. He stood with legs spread apart, feet rooted like stumps. He faced William Clark and intended only Clark to hear, but the wind amplified his voice and carried his words to every man. "What's left is for the natives and the fleas and the eternal wind and rain, Will."

"Or British traders." Clark let his words ring for all to hear: "Comowol says they'll be here in May to take possession of everything we've built." Comowol was the Clatsop chief. The month was March. Clark continued in a voice that shook with regret: "Jefferson's ship should have arrived, Meri."

Lewis ran a hand through his combed red hair and turned to face the empty buildings. As if he was alone in the world, he replied: "He dispatched it, Mister Jefferson did. I know in my bones he did. But now we must brave the dreaded Blackfeet on our way home." His thin voice fell. "And old Chief Delashelwilt will turn our fort into a brothel where his whores will sell their favors to the Brits for a gill of watered rum. May fleas and the clap infest them all." The curse was not typical of Meriwether Lewis. He frowned and added: "I've half a mind to burn it down." He laughed, but his laughter had a bitter sting.

William Clark tried to reassure. "Wet timbers won't burn, Meri. I've tacked a list of our names and exploits on the gate and given another to Comowol. American ships will come, and he'll tell them we were here, that we're alive and on our way." Clark turned to address the corps. Deliberately he infused his words with confidence for the success of the coming journey, then muttered a cursory dismissal.

The two captains walked for the last time around the empty fort, home to the corps since December 7, 1805. Its rooms were cramped, its chimneys smoky, its courtyard stubbled with rock, and its entry trampled thick with mud. Its stockade was tall and strong as the great spruce forest that surrounded it. But now they were leaving its dreary security for the wild, snowy mountains and a very distant *home*. The echo of Lewis's regret lingered. Fort Clatsop was the one place on this stormy coast where John Collins had felt safe.

Spring had barely brushed the land. Air and earth were still cool. New shoots were just beginning to emerge and snows still lay deep in the high country. The Corps of Discovery waited until noon for rainy skies to clear and for Georges Drouillard, who had gone to buy an additional canoe, to return. As the sun burned slowly through the clouds, the men sat patiently by the boats and let warmth penetrate. Gradually spirits rose. Good weather meant an end to rotting food and the coughing sickness and portended a quick and easy journey.

But Drouillard did not arrive and Collins worried. Labiche sympathized. "Give him time. Indians will bicker and cajole, refuse to sell, inflate the price."

"They might hold him hostage."

"He's too clever for that."

At midday, Drouillard appeared with two canoes, not one. He explained his delay with a sheepish curl of lip. "Traded your lace-trimmed coat, sir." When Lewis frowned, he added: "A second boat is hidden in the marshes. I stole it."

Captain Lewis's emotions snapped. "I forbade you to loot or steal. They will resent us and they will pursue." But the stormy words subsided to cynical criticism and he mumbled: "You could have saved the coat and stolen both boats." Lewis was jealous of Drouillard and of the influence he held over the enlisted men like Collins who often credited the word of Drouillard ahead of an officer's orders.

Not a wrinkle or flicker of eye betrayed Drouillard's reaction. He waited silently for Lewis to calm and for William Clark to intercede. "What else, Mister Drouillard?"

"There was a ship, sir . . . British, a sloop, three masts. They've landed a party."

Clark shrugged. "Is this a concern of ours? We know the British come to trade and have seen their wares among the natives, but they restrict themselves to the coastline. We move away from them, upriver, inland."

"They carry a swivel gun, sir, heavy armament for a trading party, and they enlist the natives in their efforts."

Clark's mild face soured. Lewis pinched his lips and nodded once to Sergeant Gass who screeched the expected order. "Climb aboard your ladies, men! Set them afloat and stroke them kindly before the red rascals discover they've been robbed." In the absence of female companionship, Gass substituted boats for women.

John Collins and François Labiche pushed the flat of their paddles into the bottom muck and the dugout moved out. Other boats, dugouts all, shoved off behind them until the little flotilla was afloat. Slowly they sailed down the Netul River to the wide Columbia estuary where a forty-foot Indian canoe blocked the channel. Its crew of twenty had come ostensibly to fish, but none was fishing now. They held the huge boat broadside to the flow.

William Clark cried loudly over the heads of his men: "Regroup! Prepare arms!" And Collins called to Labiche: "Come to take back their boats!" Labiche answered: "Furs, they think we have furs." He lay down his paddle and reached for his knife. Collins reached for his rifle.

Drouillard shouted back across the water: "They're friends, *amis*, Chinook! I took the canoe from a Clatsop beach." But he let the stolen boat drift back into the shadow of the others and they passed unharmed.

Progress upriver was exhausting and complaints loud. From the bow, Labiche shouted his displeasure back to Collins, Bratton, and York. "We plow up the river like heavy sod! Clumsy dugouts can't outrun native canoes. Grab the pole, Johnny!"

Collins shoved the pole into the gravelly bottom and pushed with all his strength while Labiche and York rowed furiously until late in the day when the light was fading and the sergeants bellowed the order to land.

A heavy mist shrouded the shore. Collins couldn't see the land as he pushed into the shallows. Bratton suddenly cried: "I smell a fire!" Collins sniffed but the sweet scent of fir masked the dry sting of smoke. Bratton's nose twitched like a rabbit's and he insisted: "Sit me up. Lemme see." York propped him higher as Bratton's beady eyes scanned the misty beach. The dugout struck bottom near a dark clump of Sitka spruce, and Bratton declared: "There they are. Behind the trees, eyein' us like a pack of wolves."

Collins followed his gaze. Snake-like shadows slinked among the trees, and coils of black smoke singed the gray mist. He dropped the pole, seized and loaded his rifle. A human form bearing a torch appeared. At first Collins thought it a mirage. He stood up and aimed as twenty Chinooks swarmed like insects from the forest onto the beach. The light of their torches illuminated chunky, brown torsos and thick, muscular arms and legs.

Gass shouted: "Sight your rifles!"

Captain Clark countermanded: "Hold your fire! They carry no weapons!"

A confounded Gass screeched: "Sir, they're lasses, fair women all!" He clambered out of the boat and into the shallows.

Labiche and a dozen men followed as the women surged forward. The bare-breasted, giggling harpies attached themselves like leeches to every available man. Chief Delashelwilt had camped here with his traveling brothel. The old pimp stood at the edge of the trees, arms folded across his chest, horse teeth glowing yellow in the torchlight, shouting encouragement to his whores as he called a welcome to the corps.

Collins called Labiche back: "Fool, the last Wasco you bedded made you scratch until you bled!"

Labiche shouted: "With this face, I take them where I find them, Johnny!"

But Collins's sturdy good looks attracted the attentions of the women and they splashed about, tugged at his clothing, and rocked the boat to unseat him. Another began to loosen Bratton's bonds.

The squatty, dirty whores disgusted Collins, so different were they from the sleek, graceful Mandan woman he loved. With his paddle, he batted them away and remained in the boat with Bratton and York. He'd suffered worse. The scars on his back, the result of an old dalliance, still itched. The women let go and he and York paddled furiously back into the stream.

Bratton's eyes stared like saucers. "I could've drowned."

Collins handed Bratton a gun. "Next time, see if you can pull a trigger."

Suddenly, from the shore, Labiche yelled: "Damn siren lifted my knife right out of its sheath!" Labiche cared for his knives like jewels in a crown and wielded them with dexterity. He dove and swam. A woman, hot on his heels, caught his ankle before he reached the boat. He rolled in the water, knocked her across the mouth, and reached for the gunwale. Collins hauled him aboard and Bratton laughed for the first time in weeks.

Vainly Captain Lewis pleaded above the din: "Do not molest them." But the words rang false. Finally even Lewis seized a woman by the hair and dragged her bodily off Sergeant Ordway. Drouillard wrapped an arm around Delashelwilt's thick neck and held his knifepoint at the jugular.

Only then did Delashelwilt call off his "daughters" and set up a ring of torches around a bright fire. He apologized profusely for the contemptible behavior of his harem and presented a pelt of a white otter to Lewis as a token of his remorse. To Clark and the three sergeants, he gave finely woven hats. He confessed that his girls preferred the Americans to the starchy British and that he could not guarantee that an assault would not happen again. With a shrug, he admitted he could not always control the enthusiasms of his "daughters".

More Indians emerged from the woods, men this time, and Labiche warned: "They send their women to distract us so their men can steal and plunder. There is the leader." He raised an arm, and Collins followed the line of his vision.

A tall man stood by Delashelwilt. His silhouette was thinner and less angular than the squatty Chinooks. He wore white man's clothing, what appeared a British officer's uniform, and stood in the light of the torches. One hand rested on a sword's gleaming hilt and the other held a dueling pistol. The light was dim, the image ill-defined. Collins narrowed his eyes in an effort to see more clearly, but the boat lurched with the current and he turned his attention to the river. When he looked back again, the man was gone. But Bratton, propped now so that he could see clearly, grumbled: "I seen the devil, Johnny."

They didn't go far. The rain resumed in heavy drops that smeared the hastening twilight. They came to an island where only the patter of raindrops broke the eerie stillness, and Bratton mumbled: "'Tis the isle of tombs. No native ventures here." They had passed the same island festooned with burial mounds on the outbound trip. For fear of ghosts, Indians stayed away. Some men feared, too, and opted to sleep in the boats, but Collins went ashore and struck a fire that he shielded from the rain with the torn square of Gibson's canvas. York laid Bratton beneath and Sergeant Pryor's mess hovered around.

Bratton would not eat, nor would he be quiet. "An Injun in a Brit navy coat with a Brown Bess rifle. Hair black as hell, face like a devil goat, wi' pointy ears an' horns, no native like we ever seen. A bloody Brit he was. I saw him plainly. Tell the captain." He stopped and challenged: "Ask Collins. Ask the slave."

York shook his head. Collins only shrugged. They had all concluded that Bratton's mind was withering along with his body. The hiss of mockery rang in Collins's reply: "Rain's damped your mind, Bratt. Brits ain't used the Brown Bess since the Revolution." No one consulted the slave.

But Bratton tossed and railed: "You're a liar, Johnny. Get Clark. Lemme talk to the captain."

On March 28th, Collins went for Clark out of pity, not duty. William Clark was eating, water dripping into his bowl from the leaky brush cover that sheltered the officers and Charbonneau, his wife, and babe. He held a bowl in one hand, a spoon in the other, but he had not touched his food. Carefully he traced their route with his spoon in the soft mud.

Collins interrupted: "It's Bratton, sir. Seein' ghosts again . . . Brit devils says he."

Clark let out a sigh, passed a weary hand over his eyes, and picked a tough slice of gristle from between his teeth. "What else did he see? The grim reaper?" He didn't try to disguise his sarcasm.

Drouillard scooped the last crumbs from his dish, and interjected: "I saw him, too." He tossed the remark like a bone to a dog and continued licking his fingers, then swallowed and muttered: "He was dark complected, part Indian like me, like Labiche, not trussed like a Chinook. He spoke English. I heard him swear." He stopped, scanned his listeners, and continued softly: "Where Britain rules, gold in a man's palm or furs in his cache buys more than spoken promises or written assurances." Drouillard raised his eyes. Bits of flame reflected in his pupils and flashed their fire directly at William Clark. "The man stood out like a swan in a gaggle of geese, sir, a mutineer, for sure, from off a Brit square-rigger." He snickered. "Bratton's right. The old pimp passed him payment. I saw."

Silence, then Meriwether Lewis demanded: "Payment for what? We've not seen a ship all winter."

Drouillard replied: "You believe only what you see, Captain? Weapons, knives, gaudy uniforms, British droppings litter this land. Gibson found a silver flask and a discarded sail. Others have buckles and buttons."

Still Lewis would not believe. "The flotsam of shipwrecks and castaways."

Drouillard shook his head. "The proceeds of commerce. Coin changed hands, the glimmer and clink of gold."

Still Lewis doubted. "The natives are well versed in commerce and trade regularly. They have Charbonneau's gold, bribes we paid to insure our own safety."

William Clark threw down his spoon, sucked in his cheeks, and thundered over the hissing fire: "Mister Drouillard suspects rightly. Bratton is sick but he's not stupid, and Mister Drouillard has the instincts of a hawk."

CHAPTER
FOUR

Two months passed and the HMS *Phoenix* returned to the Columbia estuary where she furled her sails and rocked lazily at anchor. Captain Richard Markham stood poised on the quarterdeck, one hand on the hilt of his sword, the other slipped deftly beneath the lapels of his dress uniform. The medals of his rank adorned his left breast.

As the *Phoenix* dropped anchor, another boat, a canoe filled with natives, pushed out from the shore. Ochoa stood in its bow. He wore the dress uniform coat, bicorne hat, and sword that Markham had bequeathed him. His thumbs he had tucked into his belt with a bevy of knives. With his dark complexion and array of weapons, he seemed more a swashbuckling pirate than a responsible member of the Royal Navy. But he concealed his intent: to cajole Markham out of as great a supply as possible of black powder and rum and perhaps a cannon or two.

Lieutenant Eagleton threw a rope ladder over the *Phoenix's* starboard bow and Ochoa clambered up, followed by a train of eager women. Ochoa had come to report; Delashelwilt, and his swarm of whores, to entertain. The *Phoenix's* crew had been confined to the ship all winter and hurrahed like schoolboys when the women swarmed aboard. Markham watched impassively. If he refused to admit the women, he risked mutiny.

Ochoa landed heavily on the deck and flicked a cursory greeting to Lieutenant Eagleton. Then he marched pompously to the wardroom where Markham was expecting him.

The captain was alone, seated behind the massive table. His charts were rolled and pushed to one side, and a full ship's decanter of port and two cups stood on a silver tray in the glare of the lantern that shed a halo of light in the damp, low-ceilinged interior of the wardroom. Markham did not rise when Ochoa entered but thrust his feet onto the table and signaled his orderly to pour out the port. Finally, in a voice oily and patronizing, he spoke: "Greetings, Mister Ochoa."

Ochoa's dark eyes flicked from the soles of Markham's boots to the pale blue of his eyes and beyond. He uttered the prescribed greeting and bowed slightly.

Markham was thinner, paler now after months in the northern bays. He swung his boots to the floor with the usual thump, thrust his torso forward onto his elbows, and with an index finger pointed Ochoa to a chair. His large head swayed to and fro over the table as he pushed a full cup across the table. Then he sat back, thumbed the soft facings of his coat, and spoke: " 'Tis a strange but marvelous place, Mister Ochoa, where a bedmate is more easily obtained than a glass of sweet wine." His words were slurred, his eyes shot through with blood. "How long since you've raised a civilized glass, Mister Ochoa?"

"Too long, sir." Ochoa sipped and waited. He hated the cloying sweetness of port.

The ship rolled suddenly and wine splashed like thin blood over Markham's hand. He removed a handkerchief from his sleeve, sopped up the spill, and wrung the liquid back into the cup. "I took the wine from a Spanish brig. Madeira, the very best."

Ochoa nodded. He knew Markham lied, that he had saved the rum for his own use. He smacked his lips and began confidently: "The Americans are here, sir. There are only a few of them, not enough to man a small ship. The Boston ship that was to have come to their aid some months ago left before they arrived." He added with regret: "She filled her hold with a rich cargo of furs, sir. She would have made a handsome prize."

Thought of the lost opportunity unnerved Markham. His lips pulled back in a brittle smile as Ochoa continued: "The Americans spent the winter in a swamp, sick with ague and infested with lice. Their clothing rots. Many are sick. The Boston ship will report them dead."

The captain was smiling broadly now, blue eyes glaring glassily into Ochoa's black. "Where are the traitors now?"

"In swift currents and biting winds. They've started upriver too early."

Markham's fingers drummed the hard edge of the table. He drew his lips into a needle line, closed his eyes, and pinched the bridge of his nose. Ideas bounced like dried seeds in a pod, tumbling and smashing together as Markham struggled with rational thought. Was it possible that the Americans had discovered another, warmer passage through the mountain range, a passage that Alexander MacKenzie had missed? Markham dismissed the possibility and replied: "Catch them, stop them, cut short their inquiries, blast them to splinters." Markham was clearly irritated by the news and added: "I would go after them myself but the *Phoenix* with her heavy guns cannot pursue upstream." His eyes closed. He rubbed them wearily and forced them open. "Destroy them. Do not allow them to escape."

"Never, sir. In a light, fast boat, such that the natives build, I will catch them easily. The natives are fine boat-builders, sir." He paused, exhaled, cleared his throat, and ventured: "A twelve-pounder in a large canoe would blast the Americans out of the water."

Markham squared his shoulders and drew in air to expand his broad chest. "Why a twelve-pounder? You have a swivel. Use it. I don't want a chase, Mister Ochoa. I want a killing."

"The Americans have a swivel of their own. I need a larger, more impressive cannon to win the natives to our way of thinking. And with a twelve-pounder, sir, I can assure you a more complete killing." Ochoa's brown eyes stared impassively as his thoughts raced. How to mount the large gun in an Indian canoe, keep powder dry, and Chinook thieves at bay, the efforts would be his alone. So would any booty he could seize. For now, he had only to satisfy the drunken captain with flattery and perceived obedience. He continued: "There are falls on the river, so the natives tell me. The Americans must come ashore at the base where the Indians extort a toll for safe passage. They will milk the Americans dry, then I will kill them while they sleep." He sipped his port, then added with a devilish grin: "Or we could take prisoners, trade them as inducements to the Spanish authorities. The two captains should bring a hefty reward. The others and the woman, we can let drown or deliver as hostages to the Chinook."

Markham's head jerked up. "They have a woman with them?" He blinked incredulously.

"A young girl, an Indian slave with a baby. I presume they used her to befriend the mountain tribes."

Markham closed his eyes and pinched the bridge of his nose. "No wonder the Americans falter. Bad luck, women." He drained his drink, thrust himself abruptly up from the table, and shouted for Lieutenant Eagleton, who appeared a few minutes later, disheveled and apologetic. Markham rocked on his feet, steadied himself against the table, wrinkled his nose, and commanded: "Put the women ashore, Lieutenant. Prepare to weigh anchor and hoist sails."

"Sir, they've just arrived. The men expect one night's pleasure at least," Eagleton blurted, then backed away before Markham's furious glare.

Markham smashed a hard fist on the thick tabletop, waved an accusing finger, and shouted: "Someday, Eagleton, indiscretion will be your undoing! Never dispute the orders of your captain." He slumped back into his chair.

"Aye, sir." But Eagleton lingered. "What about Chief Delashelwilt, sir?"

"Bring Delashelwilt to me, here."

Eagleton left and Markham grumbled to Ochoa: "Political appointments, they insult the worthy service of Mother England."

Silence fell and Ochoa turned to go, but Markham called him back: "Mister Ochoa, don't leave! Stay and translate." Ochoa nodded. He had learned more Chinook during his respite ashore, enough to reconfigure Delashelwilt's meaning to suit his own intention.

Delashelwilt entered and the captain offered a chair, but the Indian preferred his customary squat. Markham smiled agreeably because the chief's position on the floor inflated his own prestige. But Delashelwilt's black eyes peered intelligently at the decanter, cups, and the captain's bulging eyes that swayed in rhythm with the motion of the lantern that hung over the table. He turned his flat profile to the side, looked out the door at his departing "daughters", and cackled angrily at Ochoa.

Ochoa voiced Delashelwilt's complaint: "There was not time for his women to collect payment for their services, sir."

"Convey my regrets and tell him I will reimburse him." Markham slurred the words. To pay this ugly, groveling pimp anything at all for his prostitutes was irksome and humiliating. "Explain to him why haste is important if you are to catch the Americans, Mister Ochoa. Tell him his women are a disturbing distraction and that I must have an attentive, responsible crew." He added as an afterthought: "I'm sure it is the same for the Chinooks in these perilous waters."

Delashelwilt spat a hasty reply.

"He says you have torn his 'daughters' from their mates like babes from their mothers' breasts. He wants double payment, sir, one for services rendered and one to erase the affront to his most beautiful 'daughters'. He says you have diminished him by insulting them."

Markham's patience cracked like glass on a hot stove. He brought two fists down with a loud thud. "Double pay the devil shall have, in cheap beads, but get those harpies off this ship." Thoughts rattled in his head; in any other circumstances, he would have thrown the pimp and pilferer into the hold, nailed down the hatch, and let him rot.

But Delashelwilt was still squatting unceremoniously, grinning like a jester, and squawking demands. Ochoa translated exactly: "He'd be pleased with your blue bicorne hat, sir."

White with fury, Markham rapped the table, and sent glasses and decanter flying and spilling the wine that remained. His gaze riveted an instant on the wasted wine as he croaked: "My bicorne hat it is." He seized his empty cup, lifted it to his mouth, gulped air, and threw it against the thick planking of the *Phoenix*'s hull. The clatter rattled him even more. A loud rumble began in his chest and rose like a flood into his throat. He coughed, then cleared his windpipe, and gasped: "Another bottle, Eagleton, quickly, to settle the nerves." He rose, braced his legs, and walked to a sea trunk in a

56

corner of the room, brought out the bicorne hat, dusted it off, and held it out to Ochoa. "The hat. Give it to the conniving savage and get him out of my sight."

Delashelwilt snatched the hat and placed it on his misshapen head. It protruded from his flat brow like the peak of a gable on a steeply pitched roof. He glared at Markham and smacked his flabby lips. Sounds emerged from his mouth like the cackling of a fowl. Only Ochoa could ferret out his meaning: "He thanks you, sir. He'll send his girls up the ladders next time, as soon as you enter the harbor, for half the price."

Delashelwilt waddled out the doorway and scrambled over the gunwales and Markham fell back in his chair and closed his eyes. Suddenly he lurched forward and vomited the contents of his stomach. Then a calm settled over him and minutes passed before he looked up and muttered: "Is he gone from this ship?"

Ochoa peered out the door. "He's descending the ladder now, sir."

Markham called — "Orderly, bring a towel!" — then swept his sleeve across the surface of the table to clear the vomit and lay out a chart. "I gave you three men from off this ship. Recruit natives. Go after Delashelwilt and tell him we need men and canoes, not women. And have a look at this chart. No rivers, no falls, no flood plains, no mountains. Take your twelve-pounder. Man it yourself. Pursue the Americans. Waylay them at the falls you speak of, or wherever else." He stopped to breathe. "And take paper, quill, and ink. Draw for me an accurate map of this river and its surrounding country and this peculiar passage they call Northwest."

Ochoa pretended rapt attention, nodded agreement, and waited as Markham arched his furry brows. "Of beads and mirrors, take enough to satisfy their greed. Take powder for your guns. Take your twelve-pounder and take rum." British policy forbade disbursing rum to natives, but Markham held no scruples. "They shall have their muskets and their rum." He made a note to water it well and reserve enough for himself until he could re-supply again at Lahaina. He added: "The Americans will not expect pursuit. You may depend on the element of surprise. Use it to advantage."

"Aye, sir." Ochoa gazed down on the map and committed it to memory. The wide triangle of the estuary was sketched in black. The rest was a gaping blank. He would lose himself in that huge unknown where he would be free from the supercilious meddling of a drunken captain. He would buy his own prestige with muskets and rum. He bowed to Markham and inquired: "When and where shall I report to you the results of my efforts, sir?"

"In two months, here." Markham lied. He'd decided to set sail for the Lahaina immediately because, with the outlay to Ochoa, he was running out of rum to feed his burgeoning habit. He sat forward and with perfect British aplomb held out his hand. "God and luck go with you, Mister Ochoa."

Ochoa's sharp black eyes met the captain's self-satisfied blue, and he grasped the Englishman's hand. It was slimy with vomit, but he acceded: "And with you, sir." Suddenly Markham poured another cup, raised it, and issued a toast: "To Britain. To her conquests and to her discovery of the Northwest Passage and her just and orderly rule." He added with assurance: "Catch the traitors, Mister Ochoa. Destroy them."

Ochoa raised the wine to his lips but barely sipped. He wiped his soiled hand on the tail of his officer's coat. Even the rotting salmon in the Indian camps could not equal the stench that pervaded the low-ceilinged wardroom, and he turned and fled. The captain ordered beads and mirrors, powder and ball, and eight casks of watered rum packed into the longboat.

In the evening, after the Indians had cleared the beach and returned to their village, Ochoa rowed ashore. Parrish, the carpenter, a worthless scrapper named Douglas, and assistant armorer, Stiles, volunteered to go with him. Together they cached the trade goods under the canopy of darkness and watched the longboat return to the *Phoenix*. Then Ochoa issued his orders: "Display nothing that they covet or they will steal. We must take turns guarding our possessions until they acquire respect or fear." No one questioned his intent and they slept.

Delashelwilt was delighted with the muskets and beads. He provided six sleek canoes for Ochoa's use. One was over fifty feet long with a crew of twenty. The vessel could easily support the twelve-pounder and overtake the Americans. The gun alone was enough to enhance Ochoa's prestige, enough to dominate whole tribes. But when Ochoa mentioned installing it in the great canoe, Delashelwilt flatly refused. He wanted to melt it down for use as knives and trinkets.

CHAPTER
FIVE

As pilfering and thefts plagued the HMS *Phoenix* and Ochoa's spies, so they continued to deplete the expedition's meager stores. Every native visit meant that the corps had to guard their belongings more closely. Lewis and Clark rotated the guard regularly, night and day, and still the metallic containers and knives disappeared. Night was always the worst time. Every morning when they inventoried supplies, some other utensil was missing and only Bratton claimed to have spied the thieves. He complained loudly and insisted the captains hear him. Clark listened more to assess his deteriorating physical condition than to heed his exaggerated rantings.

Heavy raindrops bombarded the surface of the river like a million tiny pebbles when Clark came to Bratton on March 30th. Bratton lay on a pallet by a sputtering fire under the rotting sailcloth. The rain gushed off the thin canopy and smoke from the fire collected beneath. Collins and Pryor stood with heads bowed, while York rolled the sick man onto his back and shoved an arm under him to raise his head. Bratton blinked and coughed from the collecting smoke.

"Raise the canopy before the smoke sickens him more." Captain Clark lay a hand on Bratton's cold brow. "You lay flat as a puddle all day, Private Bratton, it's no wonder you can't walk."

"Smoke's thinner, breathe better close to the ground, layin' down, sir." Bratton's fingers cramped tightly around Clark's wrist. The thin thread of his voice echoed panic: "Injuns hidin' behind the trees in the raindrops, waitin' to murder us all."

Clark muttered: "Breathe too much damp, Private Bratton, makes liquid collect in your passages and visions swirl in your head." He addressed Pryor and Collins: "You men see anything?"

John Collins let Sergeant Pryor answer: "Natives comin' for salmon, sir."

Clark turned to York. "Is he eating?"

"Doin' nothin' needs eatin', massa."

"Lean him forward."

York pushed Bratton's head to his knees and pulled his shirt up his back while William Clark ran his fingers down the pasty white length of his spine. "Straight as a plumb line." The slave lay Bratton back without a word.

But Bratton eyes widened and he clung to Clark's sleeve. "I seen 'em rootin' around camp at night, like crabs, crawlin', pickin' our leavin's."

Clark rose and stepped back into the pouring rain. Blood started to pulse in his left cheek as he answered Bratton: "Natives are fishing, not hunting our hide, Private." Then he drew Collins and Pryor out of Bratton's earshot and issued his orders. "Stay by him. Talk to him. I'll send Cruzatte to play him a tune. York will bring his meals and minister to the rest of his needs."

Collins spoke for Bratton: "He doesn't like York, sir."

"On his back, he'll do as he is told, Private." Clark whirled on his heel and left.

Old Cruzatte came and plucked his squeaky fiddle. The wet strings had stretched and would not hold a tune but the music attracted activity to the place where Bratton lay.

Labiche spread a thin skin over the pasty mud and shook out his dice: "Try your hand, Bratt? Who'll cast for Bratt?"

Collins volunteered and rolled a six.

Bratton turned his face away. "No luck for me with devil eyes an' ghosts sniffin' like we was stinkin' carrion. Come sunup, disappear into the graves they come from."

Labiche muttered — "Crazy as a jaycock." — and cast the dice.

Sergeant Ordway's voice echoed over the camp: "Man the boats. Pack it all. No leavin' valuables for scavengers and thieves."

Labiche rolled the dice one last time. "Six again, Johnny, you win." He clapped Collins on the shoulder as York gathered up Bratton and they marched to the boats. They lay Bratton lengthwise in the canoe with his head resting in the black man's lap and stuffed elk hides around him.

Much had been lost, sacrificed to the inflated prices of the river natives or stolen. Collins was thankful the load was light: a few bushels of salt, knives and kettles, a basket of roots, and Bratton. With the current running against them, swelled by the snow melt from off the mountains, their efforts were great. But they set out with a song because music eased the effort.

The song was a steady, thumping rhythm timed to the sweep of York's paddle and the stab of Collins's pole. Labiche steered and piloted in the bow. Bratton's dead weight provided ballast and the dugout moved slowly upriver behind the captains' own vessel.

Days passed. The endless miles could not pass quickly enough. They left the broad estuary behind as the last days of March sped by. They traded with surly, suspicious river peoples — salt in exchange for fish, dog meat, and roots. Villages were left behind — empty ones ravaged by disease, and crowded, busy ones. Foothills shrouded in mist appeared. They masked massive, majestic mountains where clouds drooped like wet gauze over gray, jagged peaks.

April arrived, and the waters rose between the banks and impeded progress. Marshland spread wide on every side and thick fog clouded what lay beyond. Rain poured down. Water tumbled over crags, carved deep gouges in the muddy banks, and converged on the river in foaming eddies of silt and sand, burying deep the jagged rocks that only last fall threatened to gouge holes in the thick-hulled dugouts. Giant trees crashed into the stream and relentlessly the west wind swept inland from the vast Pacific. It battled the river's westward flow and pressed up huge, threatening waves. More than once, forced to stop, the corps pulled ashore and settled into a forlorn, wet camp.

At night, losses of equipment continued. Collins crowded with his messmates under crude shelters and listened to raindrops *hiss* as they hit the fire. Meat stewed tepidly, dulled to tastelessness by the admixture of rain water. Bratton complained and thinned. So did they all. Around the fire, the chatter was dull and despairing.

Bratton especially elicited harsh comment. John Colter was the first to lose his patience with the sick man. "Moans like a death wind. Like to gag 'im, let him choke." Cruzatte pointed a righteous finger and said: "Sleepin' with the black man, he's seein' black devil visions." Men nodded assent until Georges Drouillard countered: "No visions. No devils. He watches and sees whatever dwarfs an' gremlins rob us. I believe him." Because Drouillard said it, men paid attention. From Ohio, Kentucky, Tennessee, and Illinois Territory, nearly all had witnessed Indian raids in the eastern woodlands. Some harbored horrible, indelible memories and knew Indians were masters of stealth.

Collins replied testily: "We've had guards posted. They saw nothing, heard nothing."

Quietly Drouillard disagreed: "The raging waters and howling wind mask their voices, and the hard rock surfaces conceal their footfalls. We lose a paddle, a pot every night, and we blame our carelessness while they pilfer and grow rich. Bratton watches all because he lies awake. The sick man sees things our posted guards ignore. We are careless. The disappearances are small but persistent. Taken together, they create hardship." He snickered lightly. Only from Drouillard would these men tolerate the criticism. Drouillard waited and fired a dark glance at each man. When all was silent, he said: "Tonight, Johnny, you, the slave, and I, we stay awake. We watch with Bratton."

Drouillard came for Collins when darkness fell. Collins gathered up his bedding and sat beside Drouillard, next to York and Bratton. Bratton fell asleep because his complaint had been heeded, but Collins felt his own head nod and slouch against the hard muscles of the black man's shoulder. Drouillard punched him hard. "Watch. You are my witness." Drouillard and the slave never blinked.

Collins pulled his thin blanket around his shoulders and peered over the sleeping camp. Gradually the fire died and the darkness revealed only the still forms of slumbering men. Drouillard rose and stalked the perimeter. When he sat, the slave took his turn. Collins glued his sleep-tortured eyes to their hovering shadows while his mind ranged to the tall, muscular men. He thought how innately they resembled each other. In the night, both were the same dark color. Both seemed impervious to fear, mental strain, or physical hardship. Both were content with loneliness: the slave because he was a slave, unfit for the friendship of whites, Drouillard, half white, half Shawnee, highly intelligent, and a natural leader of men, because he loved the isolation of the wilds. Drouillard claimed he heard the voices of creatures of the earth. Like the slave, he prayed to some invisible spirit of creation. And both Drouillard and York contained their feelings with a stark stoicism that Collins admired and emulated.

Drouillard hardly smiled, York never. Neither did he frown. Emotion of any kind, simple approval, or dissatisfaction was absent from the slave. As an inferior being, his prayer was condemned as superstition, his overtures toward friendship rejected. He was there for others to command, to do their bidding, without judgment or response. Collins pondered the confounding question: *If York was so like Drouillard, why was he a slave? Drouillard was not an inferior being.*

Bratton rolled in his sleep. The interruption was brief but served to redirect Collins's thoughts. A movement, a shadow barely above the surface of the ground, crossed his line of vision, then vanished instantly. He rubbed his tired eyes and concluded that it was probably some small scavenger. York tapped his shoulder. His turn had come to walk the perimeter. The big black man sat. Collins welcomed the activity and arose. But the image of York, hovering over him in the darkness or on his knees praying with dark face turned to the sky, loomed like a ghostly presence. As the night wore on, Collins struggled to stay awake, he spoke to the black image: "You're a prisoner to your master, like Bratton's a prisoner to his body." He'd whispered, so he didn't think York, whose eyes had closed and whose head lolled on his chest, had heard. Collins did not speak more. The fire sputtered. It had stopped raining and there was hardly a flame. In the early dawn, John Colter joined them and Collins sat back, closed his eyes, and gave in to sleep. The ghosts that Bratton imagined had not appeared.

In the morning, when they settled Bratton into the canoe, a commotion arose in Sergeant Gass's mess. Tom Howard was missing his tin bowl and he had only a cracked wooden vessel to replace it. Howard who had a volatile temper stormed about the camp.

Captain Lewis delayed the departure and, while Howard hunted for his vessel, he summoned Drouillard, Collins, and Colter. He did not call York. He could not assign the blame to a slave. He aimed the scolding at Collins and cynicism rang in his voice: "You men were on watch. Were you asleep, Private Collins, that you saw and heard nothing?" Collins had been reported drunk on watch the second night out from St. Louis in the tiny village of St. Charles and Lewis had never forgotten although other men had been guilty of worse offenses. Sergeant Pryor, Collins's direct superior, perceived the grudge and regularly assigned Collins to duties far from Captain Lewis.

Now Georges Drouillard spoke in Collins's defense. "We were walking the perimeter, sir, wide awake, every one of us. I can vouch for Johnny. So will John Colter."

Colter nodded and Lewis did not contradict Drouillard because Colter was sure to relay news of the scolding to the corps. Men liked Collins and even the sergeants would accept Drouillard's word. But he sent a scathing glance Collins's way so that even John Colter cringed.

Collins waited with Drouillard and York who squatted on the shore near Bratton in the dugout. York sang softly to himself. The melody was haunting, the rhythm slow and mournful. When York's voice died, to fill the monotonous minutes, Collins asked: "You married?" He had rarely addressed the slave and York had never spoken to him. Now the man nodded, and Collins delved further: "You have a wife, children, a home?"

Again a nod and York began to speak: "No home. Don't own the clothes on my back, but my wife loves me like that Mandan woman loves you. I hope to God she ain't sold down the river before I git there." The comparison on the pink lips of the black slave sent shock waves through John Collins's heart.

Howard found the bowl under a rotting stump and the order to depart sounded, followed by another louder command to haul out the towropes. Paddles, poles, and tows, all were needed to counter the river's relentless flow as the expedition pushed into the gaping mouth of the Columbia Gorge. Collins pushed in the sluggish pole as York leaned his shoulders into the towrope. When they beached early, arms, shoulders, and backs ached from the strain, but their work was not finished.

While the enlisted men ate, York stirred a bowl of stew to mush and helped Bratton eat. He came back finally, and scraped the crust from the dregs of the pot and sat himself to eat with Collins, Drouillard, and John Colter. His question when it came spilled like flood water breaking its banks from his lips. He asked: "What's it like to be free?"

Drouillard stopped chewing. Collins coughed up his food, and Colter dropped his spoon. Curious glances centered on York as he resumed: "I dream ever' night, I pray God ever' mornin' for the freedom you white folks fought for. You name your children, your streets, an' your towns, *Liberty*. Out here when the wild animals call an' the wind howls, you and I are the same meat, but, where we come from, we ain't the same, never were." York's words began with a trickle, then gushed forth. "I know what you all thinkin' . . . that I could stay out here, be free like you. But I promised my wife I'd earn my freedom and hers. An' my boys . . . I sired two fine boys what lived an' two what didn't. I pray Massa Clark will remit them, too. Wind blows east ever' day, blows me closer to freedom for me an' my kin." York's eyes, sharp, black needles of light, scanned the circle for a sign of understanding and nearly every man looked away.

But Collins stared open-mouthed as a new realization took shape in his mind: for the slave, this journey was the first sweet taste of freedom. He shuddered and wondered if York had anchored his dreams to a phantom hope, or if, like Bratton's ghostly devils, they were all wandering around in this vast landscape, fabricating vain hopes and constructing impossible desires. There was no single range of mountains, no meeting of waters, no easy passage west, no boat for re-supply as Jefferson promised. Would they flounder and starve in the treacherous mountains as they had on the way out? Would the Sioux lay in wait? Would Laughing Water be waiting or would she have married another? And what of this slave who claimed a wife and mother of his children who he could never marry? Would each of them survive long enough to complete the journey? Collins hesitated, then stammered incoherently to York: "I'm not your master. Call me Johnny."

"Massa Johnny." York repeated: "Johnny." His voice was soft as down, as if his effort could blow away like fluff on a light breeze. He dropped his eyes and slowly rose to his feet. The conversation was over. He said: "Gots to tend Massa Clark an' Massa Bratton." For a man his size, his tread was as light as if his passing left only a faint vibration of earth or scattering of air, with no hope of congealing into force or consequence.

Thinking York's plight might make the sick man more tolerant of his own fate, Collins turned to Bratton.

But Bratton only grumbled into his beard: "He got two legs can walk. He can run an' save hisself from the devils that plague 'im."

Collins lingered late by the fire. To Drouillard, he concluded: "Bratt's crazier every day." When Drouillard proposed to lead a party to look for sign of human scavengers, Collins blurted: "Take York. Take the black man."

"York's needed here."

But Collins insisted: "Take him. Labiche can do for Bratton. Give the slave relief."

Drouillard requested and William Clark agreed to let York go, but with a provision: "You must bring him back." Even here, on the wild Columbia, William Clark harbored the apprehension of the slaveholder: that, given the opportunity, a slave would break for freedom.

70

Drouillard read his thoughts and replied: "He'll come back. He has a wife and two sons."

"Then leave as soon as the wind dies, at dawn. Take rifles and hunt as you go. Tell Collins to guard York." William Clark did not explain that he doubted Georges Drouillard, alone, could overpower the physically powerful slave if he tried to escape.

But Drouillard's keen instinct understood Clark's unspoken fear, and he related his thought to Collins. "Captain worries more about a slave than he does about Bratton and thieves and our dangerous way home."

CHAPTER
SIX

The wind died during the early hours, but the rain returned. The first light barely creased the night when Collins awakened and prepared to leave. The black man was already up and intoning his prayers. His voice rose plaintively, then quieted. Suddenly York approached with a kicking, wriggling Indian boy, not more than four years old. He dragged the squirming child forward by the arm. "Caught 'im when I was prayin'. He was sneakin' off wi' these." He held out the captain's bowl and fork and added: "Where do I put 'im?"

Collins rolled his blanket and fastened the wet bundle over his shoulders. He answered: "Drouillard's at the fire. See what he says. Captain's asleep."

Drouillard had stretched a skin over last night's coals to keep out the rain and was blowing the reluctant fire to life. He grinned when he saw Collins, but his face turned suddenly angry as he spied the boy in York's iron grip. He had ceased to struggle and stood quietly now, but his brown eyes were round with panic.

Collins set a kettle on and waited patiently for the water to boil. Pryor and Pierre Cruzatte arrived and dipped their cups as Drouillard remarked: "They make thieves of their smallest. That is Bratton's ghost." He turned to Pryor. "Give him to the captain when he wakes. He can bribe the mother for the return of anything else his greedy mitts have grabbed." Pryor nodded, lay hold of the boy, and bound his wrists.

Collins handed a cup to Drouillard and took a seat on a damp log. Silently the three men ate, drank, then shouldered their packs and began the hard climb out of the gorge.

Drouillard led down an ancient trail that wound through a dark primeval forest toward the steep walls of the gorge. York followed, never hesitating, never lagging. Collins came behind. The route was slippery with mud. They climbed gradually, seeking out roots and rocks and avoiding slippery moss and lichen. Collins strapped his musket to his back and used hands and feet for balance. His moccasins were torn and he stopped to line them with grass to cushion his feet.

The way steepened and thinned to a narrow slice in the earth until they could reach out on both sides and touch rock or root. The air grew warmer. Moisture, like steam in a chimney, rose from the river below. In the slant light of the rainy dawn, it created a murky soup that made vision difficult. Drouillard began to hum a lively drinking song so that they followed by sound more than by sight.

In mid-morning, the rain stopped, the clouds dispersed, and the morning sky brightened. The sun blared down, absorbing the wetness, erasing the blinding mist. York stretched out flat on his back, exclaiming: "Sun's like God's bare face an' the wind's His voice!"

They hiked to a ledge that promised a good view upriver and down. Drouillard stopped on the ledge, surveyed the valley stretched beneath them, and sat down. He pulled a hunk of dried meat from his sack, bit off a chunk, and passed the nub to Collins, who passed it to York. After eating, he drew out a *pacquet* from under his shirt and tossed it to Collins. "Use these, *mon ami*, before you become the second cripple in this corps." The bundle held a new pair of moccasins, and Collins laced them to his feet.

Soon Drouillard led off again at a furious pace, up a steep trail to the edge of a narrow headland that hung like a cornice over the course of the river. Ribbons of silvery waterfalls spilled from its heights. Drouillard lowered his sights to the river below. Collins and York followed the line of his vision and froze. A phalanx of native canoes was gliding down with the stream, graceful as a flock of geese on a pond. The boats were long and wide as the great spruces that grew along the river. Teams of rowers propelled them in the quick-flowing current with a smooth, co-ordinated rhythm in perfect V formation. Collins counted seven boats with his naked eye. Drouillard, who held the spyglass to his eye, lowered it and swore: "The whole tribe's afloat!" He passed the spyglass to Collins.

The native canoes were huge, nearly fifty feet long. Each held twenty thick-shouldered oarsmen, women in scanty capes, and naked children who knelt shoulder to shoulder. There were bows and arrows, gigs and nets for fishing, but only a few baskets of roots and several skinny dogs. Collins's hand trembled as he handed the glass to York who gave it back without looking.

Drouillard declared: "They're hungry. They couldn't wait for the salmon to arrive upriver. They bring hungry children and hollow-eyed women to intercept the fish and fill their stomachs and trade with the ships that come in the spring." He replaced the spyglass in his belt. "Wishrams, I think they are, kin to Chinooks, they don't kill. They trade."

But John Collins was not so sure and warned: "No tellin' what a hungry man will do."

They watched helplessly from their perch on the cliff as the expedition hove into view and struggled relentlessly upstream. The dugouts were spread wide like rooks on a game board. They stopped suddenly as they rounded the bend in the river and spotted the native boats. Pounded by the on-rushing current that swept the Indian vessels rapidly forward, they began to glide backwards. The men of the corps scrambled to group for defense. Their gestures and shouts carried high on the wind. Meriwether Lewis stood straight as an arrow in the lead canoe, gesticulating and waving.

York remarked: "Cap'n Lewis flaps like a frightened goose. Massa Clark knows better."

The comment drew a nod of approval from Drouillard, who grumbled: "If they had rifles and could shoot, they'd bring him down."

But the fleet Wishram canoes veered suddenly and swept quickly past and the expedition headed for land. Relief flooded the three men who watched. Collins muttered: "They could have destroyed us all. We should have stayed at Clatsop, waited for a ship."

Drouillard was quick to counter: "What ship? One of His Majesty's ships or a vessel of the Spanish Navy? Do you value your freedom, *mon ami?* Would you rather live like this man here, in slavery? Ask your friend, Labiche, what happens to a black man on a frigate, or a merchantman. You've seen the pitted skin on the pirate's back. Think of what he has endured from a Brit captain on a British Navy's ship. They use the cat-o'-nine-tails. The fate of a black man is worse. As for me, I would rather face the natives." Drouillard was part Shawnee.

Collins's ears rang. The welts of his own 100 lashes lightly laid on with a thin reed from the river haunted him even now. The humiliation had been worse than the pain.

York's brows came together. He stared out over the river and his deep tones echoed long-silent memories. "No ship for me. Never again. I counted bodies thrown into the sea. Think nobody knows. I can't forget the screams." His lips drew back across the bloodless white line of his teeth, not from fear but from anger perennially compressed. He stood like a dark pillar of stone, teeth gritted, tendons in his neck rigid and defined, staring at the native boats that were quickly disappearing downriver.

Collins clutched his rifle more tightly, pushed his wet hair back from his brow, and muttered: "Are they all there is, or are there more to come?"

76

Drouillard did not answer his question, but diverted his thoughts: "We're here to hunt."

York did not move. Drouillard drew Collins away. "He must deal with his demons alone. Leave him."

Collins contended: "We are to stay with him and bring him back." Drouillard answered: "Give him the choice, like I gave you, *mon ami*, or have you forgotten?" Collins remembered well. In the second month out from St. Louis, he had been falsely accused and summarily judged and punished. Drouillard had soothed his wounded pride, then tested his loyalty by sending him out to hunt alone. John Collins had come back.

They pressed deeper into the forest, blazing trees as they passed, but they sighted no game. Finally Drouillard stopped abruptly and directed: "Follow the riverbank. Shoot beaver, fowl, whatever will fill a hungry man's stomach. I will go inland to search for deer."

Collins watched Drouillard disappear, then struck out across a bubbling creek and hacked his way through vines the width of a man's biceps that coiled from heavy, twisting branches and snared his arms and legs. A black cloud sailed in and hovered directly overhead as thunder rolled in the distance and the wind blew cold and hard. Pintails swept in on the gusts to land on the smooth surface of a sheltered pool. Collins loaded, aimed, fired, saw a bird flap and fall. He put up his gun and hurried to retrieve his kill. Doggedly he slashed through the branches still dripping from the morning rain and stopped to check his musket. He'd forgotten to protect his rifle from the moisture. Water had fouled barrel and pan. He cursed and slung the useless firearm over his shoulder and palmed his knife. Labiche had taught him to keep it honed. The pirate knew. The knife was always a viable weapon, wet or dry, silent as night, deadly as the arm that thrust it.

He found the duck and was thrusting it into his pouch when a *crack* barely broke the threshold of sound. His throat contracted and his brain cried: *Enemy, stalker, the tiny child-ghosts that Bratton saw in the night.* More and louder cracks of heavy feet on breaking twigs followed. Carefully Collins pushed aside a drooping branch to see what creature approached. A bear cub rooted in the rain-soaked earth.

The cub had not sighted or scented him and Collins let the branch down slowly. As he glanced about for the mother, he took a step backward. Suddenly the earth crumbled beneath him. He had concentrated on the bear and hadn't noticed the ditch hidden deftly under a platform of leaves and mosses, and had fallen into the trap. The hole was damp and dark and smelled of bear. He groped for a handhold and smelled the mother's foul breath. It hugged the ground and invaded the deep trench. For a terrifying moment, he imagined the beast beside him in the trap, but she appeared suddenly above the lip of the trench, brown as a berry, with a bristling white hump at the shoulder. Her paw was as big around as the head of a man, with claws two inches long.

Collins shrank to the far corner and lay motionless as her brown eyes squinted down upon him and she sniffed his human scent. He clutched his wet rifle to his chest and closed his eyes as if by blotting out the vision he could eliminate the threat. He heard a whine, her infant calling. When he opened his eyes, she had turned away, sensing that as he was trapped, so she would be, also, if she went for him. Her offspring's cry was more compelling.

Collins drove his ear to the earthen wall, listening for the lumbering vibrations to grow weaker. He sensed a second, lighter tread and thought it the cub's, then recognized the beat of a man's feet running. He heard a scream, then a whimper. Finally, carving handholds with his knife, he clawed his way up. When he dared look, he saw the bear walking calmly away with her cub. Collins pulled himself to solid ground and stood up. The animal looked back, raised her head, expanded her nostrils, sniffed, and rose on her hind legs.

John Collins did not think. He palmed his tomahawk and drew back his arm. With all his might, he heaved the weapon. It sped through the air and struck the she-bear squarely in the shoulder. She sat back slowly and plucked it away like a sticky burr. Then she touched the place where it had struck and dabbed at the wound. Blood seeped out. She licked her fur smooth and clean. Then she caught him in her gaze and let out a monstrous howl.

Collins had struck thoughtlessly, had provoked and angered needlessly. He pulled the pirate's knife, from the hidden sheath on his thigh, ran a finger the length of his knife. The cool steel was sharp, the blade long and pointed. He prayed with all his heart that he could thrust it home before the deadly claws laid him open. He chose a tiny speck of pale hair where he thought the heart should be and took aim. But the beast fell to her four paws as he released the throw. The long knife sailed high and struck the soft meat of a spruce sapling, twanged, and hovered uselessly. The blue stone imbedded in the knife's hilt twinkled in the sun and attracted the blurry vision of the beast. But the she-bear turned, roared her outrage, and charged. Collins ran, gulping great volumes of air to feed his pumping lungs, until the cavity of his chest ached. He was still running when the shot of a musket rang out and the crashing ceased. He heard the gurgling, like water that bubbled from a spring, and turned. The bear had stopped. As he watched, blood flowed from her nose where her smelly breath had blown. She coughed and sat back. Blood pulsed out in a heavy stream from a hole in her chest. Slowly she lay back as her life poured out. Weak-kneed and panting, Collins also sat and let the panic drain from his heart.

York emerged silently from the brush, marched toward the bear, and severed the throat. He walked back to Collins and held out a hand, pulled him to his feet, and motioned him to follow.

Collins retrieved his tomahawk and knife, replaced the tomahawk in his belt and the knife in its hidden sheath beneath his leggings against his thigh, and marched off behind the slave. They came to a clearing where York slowed, then stepped back to let Collins look. He pushed aside a wet branch and said: "Not one of ours, Massa Johnny." A man lay on his back in the shade of a giant spruce. Black flies peppered the unblinking lids. The flesh of his cheek was ripped back to the bone where a giant claw had swiped. His blue coat was British and his hair was blond. His head lay at a twisted angle near a point of rock that must have punctured his skull as he fell. His coat was hardly bloodied but had been ripped away, and the pale flesh of his shoulder glowed white in the glaring sun against the blood red stripes of his wound.

York spoke softly: "She must have knocked him down, Massa Johnny, an' he hit 'is head when he fell."

They took the man's rifle and knife, powder horn, bullet mold, hat, coat, and boots. Collins gave them to York, who tied the coat around his shoulders and shoved his feet into the boots. The hat he gave back to Collins, who placed it on his head. Together they rolled the corpse into the trap hole and covered it again with the leaves and mosses.

As they worked, the curious cub watched. He was an engaging animal, about the size of Charbonneau's and Sacagawea's infant son. Collins swung his rifle, clapped, waved, and hooted to chase him away, but he would not go. Finally York held back Collins's arm, whispering: "Leave him free to come. He can do no harm." He pulled a piece of dried meat from his sack and held it out to the orphaned cub. "And thank him for sparing your life."

Thanking the spirits of beasts was an Indian custom, and Collins hesitated. He owed the slave his life, not the bear, but York would take no credit for the kill. Collins muttered his gratitude to the savage land.

They butchered the bear and cut two saplings for a travois, larger than the one that carried Bratton. They stripped bark for a harness and lined the bed with the she-bear's hide. York pulled his shirt up tight around his neck, expecting the task of pulling the travois to fall hard on his back. But Collins slipped his own shoulders into the harness and directed the slave: "Hunt. Take your freedom when it is offered. Find Drouillard. Don't hurry back." With a defiant grin, he took a step forward, muttering: "Could use a good horse." York nodded obediently. Slowly his dark face broadened in a wide smile as Collins began the steep descent to the river.

CHAPTER
SEVEN

The game trail, that Collins descended, fell away steeply, then sliced the thick forest to the river below. Going down proved a greater challenge than climbing up. Collins reversed the travois, braced his strength against the weight, and let gravity pull the heavy load down. He diverted his eyes from the frightening sight on the river and sought only the next footfall. The cub followed. Collins waved it away, but the animal merely shadowed him at a greater distance.

When he came to the ledge where he, York, and Drouillard had spotted the native canoes, he stopped to catch his breath and dared look down. The expedition was still camped on the sandy shore where they had retreated only yesterday. Now the ribbon of river was crowded with boats. Indians were arriving from upriver and down. There were large vessels and smaller, plainer skiffs. Many were carved with fanciful animal images. One was a large coastal vessel with the high, fan-shaped bow the Chinooks built to disperse volumes of surf. Collins marked it distinctly even at this great distance. When he'd worked at the salt-making, he'd seen many such boats ram through the crashing Pacific breakers in an effort no white man would dare.

Now Indians disgorged from the boats, hailed their kinsman with hoots and cheers, and threatened to engulf the expedition. The corps raised no defense. Indians, a few in the soiled whites of British seamen, clambered about setting up square, mat lodges. They carried a variety of knives and cutlasses that hung in scabbards at their waists. Some were armed with simple clubs, but a few held muskets. Their women and children had set up cook fires with large iron cauldrons boiling in the shadow of the expedition's dugouts. A flying spark could ignite a boat and every Indian gazed on the corps with owlish, envious eyes.

Collins slipped farther down the trail. What he saw appalled him and he tugged the brim of the dead man's hat over his eyes. The corps was scattered haphazardly about the beach in tiny blocks. Their clumsy dugouts appeared like skinny nags on a string. As he watched, the outnumbered white men gathered against the burgeoning throng and formed a broad arc to protect the boats. In their haste, they left kettles, salt, powder, and ball lying on the open beach. Naked children romped over the goods.

"Fools, where are your eyes?" Collins cursed, and spat. To him, the ploy was obvious. He muttered again: "It's not capture you should fear, it's theft." But words could not quell the terror rising in his throat. He fished a cartridge from his pouch, bit off a charge, and rammed it home. But as he leveled his sights on a native heart, he stopped. The tall figure that focused his gaze wore the blue coat of a British ship's captain. It nipped smartly at the waist and defined a lithe, athletic build. A shiny red bandanna held the man's black hair beneath a plumed, bicorne hat. He looked like a dashing buccaneer, dark like Labiche, but more muscular and fully formed. Two other men, dressed in seaman's whites, accompanied the dark man. Collins focused the spyglass on a taller, spidery form, then swung it away to another shorter and wispy silhouette. The tallest one in the officer's coat was clearly the leader. His bold swagger and length of stride distinguished him from the shorter natives as he marched with blatant arrogance, toward Meriwether Lewis and William Clark. A train of attendants followed in his wake as the disheveled, disorganized rabble parted before him. A line of Indians deployed in front of the corps as he paraded to the fore. It was an impressive scene and subtle diversion. Another line wedged behind the corps toward the boats. Veiled in pomp and confusion, the men at the scene did not perceive it.

From where Collins stood, the native intent was clear. He screamed into the wind: "Wolves have their teeth at your throats and you don't know enough to cower." With trembling fingers, he cocked his rifle and pulled the trigger. The flint snapped dully. The pan was still wet. Frantically he released his harness, leaped to the front of the travois, and cascaded over deadfall and rock. The travois bounced behind him. He stopped once, cupped his hands to his mouth, and shouted till his lungs pumped dry, but the clamor on the beach drowned the volume of his cry.

He started again, and now the travois threatened to overtake him. He dug in his heels, leaned his whole weight to resist its force. He gave a hard heave backwards, then felt the travois heave. It careened down the rocky slit, pulling him straight toward the crowded beach. Indians and whites heard the crashing brush and scrambled out of the way as travois, carcass of bear, and a battered John Collins came to rest in a heap. Instantly Indians closed in around him. He pulled himself to a sitting position, licked his lip, tasted salty blood, and swiped an arm across his mouth to staunch the flow. He was dizzy and scratched, but whole. He dropped his hand from his face and his bloody fingers landed inadvertently on the thick fur of the she-bear. The gesture was involuntary, but the natives saw it as a sign of dominion over the beast they feared most, and drew back in awe.

A hundred hungry eyes focused on Collins. Here was meat enough to fill the stomachs of every man, woman, and child, meat fallen into their laps like spring melt from off the mountains. Here was an end to the winter's starvation.

As Collins shook himself loose from the broken harness, Labiche shouldered his way through the crowd. He grabbed Collins by the shoulders and propelled him toward the safety of the corps. Collins didn't glance back. Suddenly he was without York, the slave he'd been assigned to guard, groping for a likely excuse, stammering breathlessly face to face with Captains Lewis and Clark. He pulled the dead man's hat from his head and thrust it forward. "Took it from a white man, a Brit, I think." He added belatedly: "Sirs."

Lewis took the hat, examined it, and handed it back. "And where would he be, Private?"

"Dead, sir. The bear killed him."

"A bear killed Captain Clark's slave?"

"No, sir." Collins, who could quickly spring to the defense of a friend, blundered his own defense. He shook his head, then nodded as if to shed the thought of the terrible clawing that could have been his. "The dead man wore the hat, sir. York's ball downed the bear, but she'd already killed a man. I took the hat so you'd know. York has his rifle, coat, and boots. He made the kill, then went for Drouillard."

Lewis eyes shot darts. "So I'd know what, Private? I ordered you never to leave the slave." Collins was not a favorite. In Lewis's estimation he was too often disobedient, prone to interpreting orders to suit his own whim, more likely to follow the counsels of Drouillard or the weaker dictates of the other officers. Lewis looked down his nose and inquired acidly: "Have you a witness besides yourself and a slave that the man was not Indian and was in fact white? Did Mister Drouillard see the corpse?" Collins remained silent. In no way could he make Lewis believe him.

Clark took the hat, fingered the soft felt, and eyed Collins through narrowed blue eyes. "If York does not return, Private, I will hold you responsible with Mister Drouillard." Then he addressed Lewis: "It's British, a seaman's wear. Perhaps the merchant ships have already arrived for the spring trading season. I see no reason to doubt this man or my slave, when he returns." But he repressed the sarcasm and pointed. Collins recognized the man in the blue naval officer's coat who he had seen in his gunsights as Clark questioned: "A coat like that one?" He pointed straight at Ochoa.

Collins replied. "Aye, sir, but the dead man was white."

Lewis folded his arms and rapped nervous fingers against his bony elbows and refused to follow Clark's designation. He sputtered: "Impossible."

But Clark continued calmly: "The bays are filled with backwaters and nooks, Meri. A ship could easily have landed a party and mutiny is always a possibility. Labiche will avow to that." To Collins, he murmured: "You are dismissed, Private. Go while you have the chance."

Collins stood firm as Sergeant Ordway interrupted: "Sirs, the head man wants to meet you."

Meriwether Lewis and William Clark followed Ordway to meet the tall head man. Lewis stopped when he saw Ochoa in the British coat. "He's Indian, Will. He'll want bribes. He's not a fool."

"Then bribes we'll give and escape with our lives."

"We have only salt and the hide and carcass of a bear. Our men are hungry, too."

Together, they stepped forward to meet the strange head man. He was nearly as tall as Clark's six feet and met the captains eye to eye. Lewis made the only acceptable offer — bear meat and the salt to preserve it, in exchange for safety and escape. Lewis formed the words in broken Chinook and blanched in shock when the tall Indian answered haughtily in perfect English.

Ochoa's piercing eyes flicked over the corps, recording clothing, boats, bushels of salt, canisters of powder, and condition of weapons in a steel-trap memory. What he saw pleased him. The Corps of Discovery had few possessions. Their buckskin clothing was poorly tanned, stitched, and pieced together in whatever pitiful design the skin of the animal dictated. On the social scale of the river valley, they ranked well below the leaders of tribes, below sea captains and the crusty seamen who manned tall ships, beneath the poorest Chinooks. Collins, who they believed had killed the bear, was greater, because the feat inspired admiration and awe.

A great clamor echoed suddenly from the crowded beach, followed by complete silence. The cub had braved the throng to find its mother. He stood tall and erect on his stubby hind legs, atop her corpse. At the same moment, York arrived. The natives drew back at the sight of the black man who seemed a personification of the dead bear. But the head man was not fooled and scrutinized York's physique as a horse trader would appraise the musculature of an animal for sale.

Labiche saw the leer and muttered to Sergeant Pryor: "Sir, he's no Indian. He knows the worth of a strong man slave on a Spanish block. We are the objects of his scorn. First he must feed his followers. We must go, and go now. Alert the captain."

Ochoa smiled and William Clark smiled, too, as Pryor repeated the warning. He ordered an immediate departure.

Ochoa accepted the bear in payment, and the hungry Indians swarmed over the meat thick as flies to carrion. Children gathered firewood and kindled fires. The women set to butchering on the spot. In minutes, they had apportioned the entire animal. Hungry children ate the bear flesh raw, while the corps backed warily toward the waiting boats.

Ochoa let them go. Time and the instinctive native acquisitiveness he would use to advantage at a later date. For the present, the bumpkin Americans could be left unchallenged. Theft and subterfuge better served his purpose.

The corps tossed possessions pell-mell into the dugouts. In a feat of strength, Labiche carried William Bratton over his shoulder, dumped him in, and jumped aboard. Collins raced to untangle lines and push the boat into the shallows as York splashed up beside him. The command to shove off followed immediately, but Collins drove in the pole and refused to allow the boat to enter into the channel. "Drouillard's still out!" he shouted frantically. Lewis screamed for him to depart. Defiantly he shouted back: "Not without Drouillard!" Other boats launched and moved off quickly, but John Collins held his lonely boat back.

He sighted Drouillard sprinting onto the beach and disappearing in a throng of natives. He reappeared, casting Indians aside, running like a fox for his hole. As he reached the water's edge, he pitched his rifle to

Labiche and heaved himself into the air. He landed with a splash on the surface of the water and swam. In three powerful strokes, he gained the boat where Collins pulled him in by his rope belt and the braided hair of his head.

They stroked wildly to catch up with the rest of the corps. When finally they floated safely in midstream, they looked back to see that no one followed. The river was flat as a puddle and empty. Drouillard pitched a dripping *pacquet* at Collins. It landed on the hardwood hull and split open. The bear's teeth and claws with some flesh still attached clattered out like tossed dice. Drouillard exclaimed: "They're for you, Johnny! Wear them with pride!"

But Collins ignored the prize and shouted back: "Give them to York! He killed the brute!" Paddling with every ounce of his strength, he let the trophies lay.

It started to rain, first a few scattered drops, then heaven poured out its wrath. Thunder cracked and lightning rent the darkening sky. Sheets of rain clouded their vision but made pursuit difficult. The corps rowed frantically upriver, through the billowing storm. As light began to fade, exhaustion and pain took their inevitable toll. Men would have to stop soon to eat and sleep and recoup lost strength. Bratton cried out for nourishment, but they rowed on.

Late in the evening, they landed and started a fire and York held his new coat to the light and tried it on. The corps gathered around and fingered the smooth wool and velvet facings. It had been a year at least since many had touched woven cloth, but they stood back when Meriwether Lewis entered the circle. He, too, stroked the finely woven cloth and settled a disdainful gaze on Collins who had refused to obey his command.

"British, you say? A white man's? Is this another of Bratton's visions? We are the only white men on the river." A wave of anger swept from Lewis's neck, to his downturned mouth and the pinch of his narrowed eyes. He waited, tried to contain his wrath, then drove his point like a nail into rain-soaked wood. "We have a cripple and a woman and a child to care for, Private Collins. Please confine the constructs of your capable imagination to the campfire and its gossip." Lewis's head wobbled and his pupils contracted. Captain Lewis had driven and encouraged his little group all the way to the Pacific, but now that they were a cohesive and dedicated corps inured to the hardships of the trail, now that they were headed home, worry and exhaustion nibbled at the fringes of his brain. He had not found a Northwest Passage and he could not dismiss the possibility that he, and the expedition he captained, could still fail. He paused, blinked, and addressed the slave. "Indians wear uniforms that British traders discard or barter. Did your master try the coat? It would become him. And what of the rifle?"

York slipped his arms compliantly out of the sleeves and handed the coat to Lewis.

Collins was about to protest when Drouillard lay a staying hand on his arm and counseled: "You will only irritate the captain more. The slave knows you meant it for him."

"Then give this to the captain." Collins pulled out the pouch that contained the claws and teeth of the bear.

"Give them to the slave. It was your life he saved."

"I offered. He would not take them."

That night, before he slept, Collins offered the treasured remains again to York, and again York refused the gift, but this time with an explanation. "I am a slave, without rights to ownership. I am the property of another. Give them to me when I am free."

The coat did not fit William Clark and he passed it on to Charbonneau who handed it back to York with an admonition: "Hide it. Spirit it away."

The next day, April 7th, at dawn, William Clark gave the order to depart and hasten east upriver as fast as possible. They struggled past rocky crags and mountaintops crowned white with snow. Lewis distanced himself from his men, who turned for affirmation to the steadier William Clark and Georges Drouillard. Only a faint semblance of discipline endured: the daily inspection and call of the roll. But after two years of travel, each man knew his duties and performed them competently without direction. They had fled from cold, wet, starvation, and mountains, but never before had they run from men. A human enemy threatened and so they pushed inexorably on. Fierce winds from the west hammered them east, toward the cold and starving mountains, away from the thieving hordes of the river valley.

Drouillard, followed on foot, setting his own grueling pace and guarding their backs. He avoided Meriwether

Lewis and entered the camp only when he had meat to bring, usually no more than stringy elk, or some pertinent news for William Clark. He stayed out for intervals that increased in duration until Captain Clark feared that he had succumbed to the impulsions of his Indian heritage, and he sent Collins and Labiche to bring him in.

They found Drouillard happily cleaning his knife, alone, squatting on his heels, Indian fashion, by a tiny rivulet. He saw them before they saw him, and he displayed his kill, two fat bucks. The meat lay on a flat rock in a pool of blood. Drouillard rubbed his biceps and called out: "If I'd entered the camp with such quantities, they'd stuff it raw into their mouths, sicken and slow! My arm is stiff from butchering. Sit, *mes amis*, and we'll cook and eat our fill." He smiled and the hard lines of his face eased. Smiling, he was a strikingly handsome man. "We'll pack it in tomorrow and tell Cruzatte to tune his fiddle." He unfolded his crossed legs, reached out, and sliced off a chunk of raw liver. "The best part, the Indians say." He stuffed it into his mouth and wiped his bloody lips on his sleeve. Collins and Labiche laughed and ate their share.

In the morning, the three men hauled the venison back to camp. Cruzatte fiddled and John Colter danced with Labiche as the corps fell ravenously on the fat meat. Labiche, the pirate, proposed a toast: "To good fortune and good health. May the best of our days that are past be the worst of our days to come." And Drouillard added: "The wind is with us, *mes amis*. Manitou smiles." He struck Collins playfully in the

94

small of his back and pronounced: "Love blossoms, *mon ami*. It is spring."

Spring was beautiful on the river. Trees and vines were sprouting and animals were fattening fast. Black, indigenous deer romped the lush forests. Beaver and fish abounded in the rivers, fowl in the air, and the salmon would soon fill the waters. Hunting improved and with it the appetites of men. But Meriwether Lewis ate only sparingly. John Collins strung the bear's teeth and claws on a leather thong that he wore around his neck. He would give it to York when the captain set him free, or, if York permitted, he would give it to Laughing Water with his apologies and plea for reconciliation.

CHAPTER
EIGHT

The encounter with the Wishrams disappointed Ochoa. Their insatiable hunger and capricious superstition spread like a fast flame to his loyal Chinooks. But Ochoa blamed himself as much as the unsuspecting natives and set about devising schemes to use their impulses to assure his own ascendancy on the river.

The Chinooks had welcomed him and regaled him with gifts. He'd hired scouts among their best boatmen and worked his way inland. He explored and mapped as he went and impressed the various tribes with his clothing, whiskey, and twelve-pounder cannon. But he was islander and seamen, as were Parrish, Douglas, and Stiles, the three men from the *Phoenix*. Now Stiles was gone, disappeared in the vast forests. Douglas and Parrish were left, and they were seamen like him, not woodsmen or rivermen. They knew only wide bays, tides, deltas, the gaping mouths of rivers and deep-drafted, ocean-going vessels. Yet they elected to pursue the Americans the way they knew best, by water, on the wild rivers. Falls, whirlpools, caving banks, shifting bars, and the vagaries of inland waterways were to them unknown, and the vessel they built in a quiet cove where the estuary narrows to meet the river was not well suited to the mighty Columbia.

The design, sketched by Parrish the carpenter, resembled more an ocean-going ship than a standard native canoe. Its construction, by the coastal Chinooks, cost time and effort and further delayed any pursuit of the Americans. But such a vessel impressed the natives greatly. And now the fishing season, when the salmon were expected to arrive, was upon them.

Ochoa paid dearly for the laborers he needed but results exceeded his grandest expectations. The Chinooks were superior boat builders and modified Parrish's sketches to suit their peculiar whims. They constructed a huge canoe emblazoned at the bow with the giant, carved head of a raven. The bird's eyes were the color of flame and its hooked beak loomed black and predatory. Parrish set a platform and bored a hole behind the beak where he placed the cannon. He inserted the mouth of the gun into the hole. He winked when he showed his handiwork to Ochoa: "Don't need a ball, just powder to crash an' shake their bloody ears, an' flame to spout from the dragon's mouth. They'll think you a greater god than Markham worships." When the gun went off, ball, flame, and billows of heavy smoke issued from the beak in a thunderous roar. Parrish laughed and added: "I call her the *Devil's Bird*."

Parrish's assessment proved true. The natives assigned totemic power to the boat whose beak spit its magic on Ochoa's command. They already worshiped the great raven who flew on the updrafts above the clouds, whose giant face some ancient hand had carved on a high promontory over the river. It was a broad visage, wider than it was long, with glaring hemispheres of eyes that peered into the bottomless depths of the river. The bird's beak had chipped away long ago and left a hideous cavern of mouth. The effect was a predominance of eyes that resembled a glaring, ceremonial mask. No one ventured on the sacred mountain, and, when they traveled on the river beneath the image's glare, they spread offerings on the waters. So, too, no one dared approach the twelve-pounder in the bow of Ochoa's boat.

The day arrived in the month of April when Ochoa reached a narrowing of the river. The hulking vessel did not maneuver well where the river narrowed and the currents converged in the great gorge. Swift rapids forced him to stop, find a mooring in a quiet cove, and come ashore. But the cove was noisy and active. A large village was there and he fired a double charge to announce his arrival. The gun boomed, spat its orange flame, and coughed up black smoke. The tribal elders cowered. Ochoa disembarked to hushed voices and terror-stricken faces. Many inhabitants had abandoned their huts and fled to the safety of the surrounding rocks. They called out to their god to protect them. Others brought gifts to silence the god. And some avowed Ochoa was a devil and Douglas and Parrish, his mischievous servants.

Ochoa reveled in the attention. Quickly and easily he assumed the aspects of men of power, gods, and masters who he had distantly observed: the clam-eyed judge who'd sentenced him to fifty lashes with the barbed cat-o'-nine-tails and life in a Cuban jail; the greedy jailer who sold him as a black man for twenty guineas to a Spanish brig's captain. He dismissed the benevolent, humble half man the Christians called Jesus and he knew little of the Manitou, the creator god of the tribes. He patterned himself, instead, on the just, wrathful god of the Hebrews. Markham's stilted British speech and haughty airs were especially fresh in his mind because Ochoa owed his freedom to Markham and the men of the *Phoenix* who had seized the Spanish brig and set him free.

He directed a high throne be built in an arbor from which he could preside. The natives covered it with rich otter pelts. He stretched Markham's blue navy coat over his broad shoulders and buttoned the white ruffled collar of his shirt halo-like about the olive skin of his neck. The shiny sword of command he hung against his thigh and a pistol in its holster he buckled around his waist. Chin uplifted, right hand over his heart, he sat on the throne and posed as he had seen admirals pose.

Chinooks, Skilloots, and Wishrams, who gathered at the riverbank for the spring salmon run and their annual river rendezvous, marched to greet him. They laid exquisite ermine pelts and baskets of freshly caught fish on the ground at his feet. Elders offered baskets of roots and stacks of woven, conical hats and women. Ochoa loved women and accepted eagerly. He watched them at their daily tasks, collecting wood, building fires, and erecting lodges of plaited mats, and chose only the most appealing. They welcomed his advances.

The squat men, honing their gigs and mending their nets, did not seem jealous. They bowed when he passed. Clearly the business of fishing was all-important and held them captive to the river. No amount of cajoling could shake them loose from their toil and persuade them to chase Americans upriver.

And so Ochoa lingered. Life was comfortable and easy. Days and weeks slipped by and Ochoa lost interest in the Americans' presence. Soon even their arms ceased to tempt him more. If he needed arms, he could find them easily among the villagers, so his Indian guides assured him.

So Ochoa joined the native fishermen and curried the favor of the chiefs. He presented head men with muskets and other leaders with mirrors and finger rings inlaid with stones. To their wives, he gave strings of blue beads, and to the younger women he courted, mirrors to reflect the flattened images of their faces. The pistols were defective, the stones, colored glass, but Ochoa was careful to explain their powers: "The cloudless sky and the waters under the sun's clear light will shine forever from these jewels that will adorn you. As fire belches from the mouth of the raven, so this gun will assure the salvation of your people." The speech was an exaggeration, the promises hollow, but his eloquent tones resounded and inspired. He had a flair for language and an instinctive grasp of the native mind and had worked hard to master their jargon.

The elders reciprocated by declaring a feast in his honor. Entire tribes came forward to regale him with food, horses, and more women to answer his smallest

100

need. He returned the horses. He was afraid of the beasts and had never ridden one. But he ate the food, bedded the women, and passed them on to Douglas and Parrish. The Indians built him a house on the shore of a narrow backwater that emptied into the cove where the great canoe, the *Devil's Bird*, was moored.

The feasting continued unabated for days. Women came each morning with gifts and food. Then the elders came. Ochoa accepted all and distributed the bounty to petitioners whose numbers continually increased.

Only one wiry little shaman challenged him. He slinked into Ochoa's house as the sun's first rays penetrated the cove. His black eyes were spaced widely apart, his nose spread pasty and flat across his moon face, and his expanse of forehead shone like polished mahogany. He was naked except for the customary truss of the Indians of the tidewater. He came soundlessly into the lodge and pushed back the partition that veiled Ochoa's bed.

Ochoa was sleeping soundly on velvet-smooth skins with an arm draped over his companion of the night when the shaman flipped back the cover and pulled the woman up without warning. Ochoa sat bolt upright and struck out, but the little man folded to dodge the blow. He carried a basket with a lid tied down, the repository of his spells and potions that he set squarely before Ochoa, and he spoke in a shrieking treble: "If you are a god, why do you bring us *mamook halo?*" Ochoa met the black eyes with an angry glare as he struggled for meaning.

The shaman continued his harangue in a flood of syllables that shot from his lips like the blasts of a tin horn. "*Mamook tumtum* no god! *Tumtum* you *olo* hungry. *Tumtum* eat all my people have, all they can catch in the river, and still you not satisfied. A devil is what you are, the *mesachie* wind who blows in from the ocean of the north and only takes the shape of a man to satisfy his greed!" The shaman's voice rose in a wailing crescendo that awakened everyone who slept in the lodge and ended with a curse: "You are no man. Like your great canoe, you are a devil, like all the rigged ships that spit fire and spread sickness and death. I will flail the skin from your back, melt your bones, and chase your spirit on the east wind across the sky, beyond the bottomless sea."

Ochoa eyed the man with a cold stare. He reached for his white ruffled shirt, pulled it over his head, slipped his legs into his breeches, and his arms into Markham's coat. As he dressed, he devised his schemes. His presence, it seemed, was costing the tribe dearly. The season's supply of food was diminishing rapidly. Men drunk on his watered rum were shooting rifles and chasing women and had abandoned the sacred effort of harvesting salmon. There would not be enough food to sustain the village until the next run of fish.

But the words registered a singular thought in Ochoa's fertile brain — that the shaman must be silenced and that he must be absolutely certain of his dominance over the tribes. He closed his eyes and contemplated how best to discredit this man. Softly, in an even monotone, he replied: "I have done you no harm. I have brought you gifts of knives, rum, and guns."

The shaman cackled and scrambled to his feet. "Get up. Come. We talk." He moved to the fire where he spread a skin on the cold lodge floor, retracted his limbs into his customary squat, and motioned Ochoa to a place at his side.

Ochoa shoved a knife into the sheath at his waist and stalled. He was the interloper who must sort the shreds of reason from the shaman's diatribe. Priests like this shaman coveted the devotion of the people, and like the Pharisees, who accused the Christ, so this shaman would betray Ochoa.

Ochoa breathed deeply, then drew himself to his full six-foot height and walked with aplomb to the place opposite the shaman. He avoided the skins and sat on the bare earth facing the man and filling the width of his vision.

The shaman removed two sticks and a round stone from his basket, placed the stone in the coals of the fire, and manipulated it with the sticks. When it had heated to shimmering red, he removed it and raised his voice. "If you are a god, it will lie cool upon your tongue and you will swallow it like a sweet berry."

Ochoa laughed uproariously until the little man averted his eyes, then he declared: "You would silence a god's voice with a stone?" He laughed again louder and chose words to equal the shaman's threat: "I will breathe ice upon your foolish stone and rain down the north wind upon your people. I will toss your potions to the clouds and dash them against the granite walls of mountains. Your gods will flee far from your villages and dance on the updrafts of the coming storm. There, they will shut out the sun forever and sickness and death shall reign among your people." While the shaman listened, he scratched a pebble from the earth and hid it in the crease of his palm. When he finished, he smiled. The speech had frightened the Indian. It had sounded Biblical, like the sermons Captain Markham delivered Sundays on the *Phoenix*. Finally, without flinching, Ochoa picked up the hot stone, by a sleight of hand exchanged it with the cold. He dropped the hot and placed the cold in his mouth, lodged it in his cheek, and swallowed. He cast a glance at the face watching and exclaimed: "You are the shaman! You decide what I am!"

The shaman's black eyes retracted in shock into their sockets. He knew he had been duped, but he had not seen how. He collected the implements of his magic and placed them back in his basket, rose, extended a skinny arm, and pointed a bony index finger in Ochoa's face. "You English. You liar. Damn to hell."

Ochoa replied impassively: "I'm not English. You don't know who I am." He watched the shaman retreat. When he called Douglas and Parrish to his side, he did not mince words. "Gentlemen, the *Devil's Bird*, which has served us so admirably in the estuary, will flounder like a sick bird in the narrow river. In the heavy wind and narrow passages, our sail is useless. We can pursue the Americans as Captain Markham intended, for what little booty and few weapons they have, or we can remain here as lords and masters."

Douglas, the youngest, objected: "We were to meet the *Phoenix*, sir, go home." Douglas was a coward who had heard the Americans had 100 armed men, muskets that never missed their target, and a magic gun that shot wind without smoke or sound. Worse he was addicted to rum. Ochoa would be well rid of him.

Ochoa flashed a benevolent smile. "You shall meet the ship, Mister Douglas. But these fickle natives are proving unreliable, unequal to the task assigned. I fear good Captain Markham has not comprehended their limitations. Sleep on it, Mister Douglas. We'll talk in the morning."

Events did not wait for morning. A *crack*, like splitting wood, interrupted their conversation, and Ochoa slid his knife from its sheath.

"That's for us, mate." Parrish moved stealthfully to the doorway, drew back the flap, and peered out.

A group of Indians had massed in the oncoming darkness. Their silhouettes hovered black against the purple sky of evening. The Indians kicked and poked at a bundle on the ground.

Parrish called: " 'Tis a man they've seized an' they've pulled him down!"

The crowd of Indians stepped over the crumpled body and marched forward, two by two. They stopped in front of the lodge and called out Ochoa by name.

He stepped uncertainly into the twilight.

A hunched man, leaning on a staff, limped forward and knelt submissively on one knee, then straightened stiffly. He stretched out the left hand, palm up.

Ochoa recognized the gesture of friendship and sent Parrish to examine the downed man.

The rapid speech that spilled from the old Indian was difficult to decipher. "She Who Watches from the high cliff where the raven meets the rain clouds has snuffed out your enemy and ours." Ochoa held up a hand to slow the harangue, and the old chief resumed in halting spurts. "This man has insulted our new god who comes from the sea. We reject him and ask forgiveness for his error." The chief bowed his head and the men behind lowered their eyes and rocked back on their heels.

Ochoa snatched only partial meaning until Parrish called back: "'Tis the shaman, sir, killed by the hand of his own people!"

The murderers were proud and unrepentant. They bowed and the movement spread like a lapping wave through the crowd. Ochoa puffed out his chest, pulled himself to his full height, and basked in his new importance. When the Indians carried away the corpse, he turned to Douglas. "They will have an escort to accompany you back to the *Phoenix* in the morning."

CHAPTER
NINE

As the corps moved upriver, the anticipated pursuit did not materialize. They pushed through the gorge of the Columbia to a place where tremendous cliffs crowded the waters that converged in a giant chute and crashed down over bare rock to a quiet pool below. Here fish collected and here the press of humankind, awaiting the return of the salmon, was thick. Natives crawled over every rock, crevice, and length of beach, built platforms that jutted over the river, mended nets, sharpened gigs and skinning knives, and fashioned hooks of bone and bark. Their fishing perches jutted dangerously over the stream. Scavenger birds hovered overhead and bears came awaiting the feast. Men, women, and children, old and young, gathered for the harvest from all the lands drained by the river and waited for the fish that would arrive very soon.

A single silvery fish signaled the beginning of the run. Great schools followed until the pool boiled to overflowing with silvery bodies flinging and flipping themselves up the treacherous rocks against the relentless flow. The Indians caught them with hooks, gigs, weirs, and their bare hands. They hauled the flapping fish out of the river, skinned and boned and hung the pink meat to dry. Women boiled the flesh and pounded it to fine powder, palmed it into cakes, and filled every storage basket to brimming. And they sang and danced and feasted on the sweet meat.

Word of the god-like head man in the *Devil's Boat* spread quickly through the population of the river. Rumor inflated with each telling until Ochoa's arrival became an event infused with fear and awe. But the *Devil's Boat* did not arrive. Instead, the bumbling Americans came, in their rotting skins and leaking dugouts, carrying their sick and exhausted, slogging through the river, upsetting weirs, overturning platforms, and invading precious fishing space with their camp.

"Get a horse." The jibe echoed sarcastically from various members of the corps. Drouillard silenced the call: "The only horses on the river are nags and cripples." Drouillard had spied horses daily as he hunted the surrounding valleys and he related his sightings to the sergeants and to Collins and his messmates. Horses would mean an end to blistered feet, aching shoulders, and the endless struggle against the mighty river.

Other men besides Drouillard had spied horses, too, and agreed that they were all skinny, unhealthy beasts. They stood at the edge of the forest, heads drooping, bony rumps tucked to the wind. Only Lewis greeted the sight with enthusiasm and exclaimed to William Clark: "I've prayed for the day, Will, when we can ride overland, past the dreadful falls and rapids and away from these thieving denizens of the river!"

Lewis's hopes were premature. The Wahclella nation, who possessed the horses, were even cannier traders than the Chinooks. They agreed to exchange horses for guns and kettles, then recanted. One demanded Lewis's Newfoundland retriever for a sway-backed mare. He explained he ate dog and relished the taste of fat dog meat. When Lewis refused and the dog disappeared the next day, Meriwether Lewis flew into a fury. "Shoot, if you must, but bring the animal back alive." Labiche caught the thief and held a knife to his throat. He released the dog.

On April 8th, a Tuesday at dawn, John Collins awakened to sunlight stabbing him in the eyes. It glanced in bright swaths off shimmering hills. Rain was a distant memory as York's voice sang over the camp.

Collins threw his blanket back and poked Labiche awake. "Get up. The slave's prayin' an' the sun's high."

Bratton muttered: "What's he prayin' for? He can paint his face white before God minds his prayers. Even free, some greedy slaver'd snatch him up an' haul him off to Cuba for sale."

Collins replied: "Prayer like his is hard to deny. Cap'n Clark is a fair man."

But Labiche countered: "Fair enough to us, not fair to his slave."

In spite of good weather, departure was delayed. Waiting men gathered eagerly around a low breakfast fire, but York ate alone because his growing assertiveness had aroused a chorus of criticism.

"Slaves ain't supposed to pray."

"Not in public where a white man can hear."

"That what he's doin', prayin'? Claps and squirms like a worm on a hook."

And Cruzatte, self-appointed moralist of the group, declared: "He has no place with good Christian men. The blood of Abel rests on his soul."

Labiche laughed and decried Cruzatte's overblown zeal: "God punished Cain. York's a man who wants his freedom like Bratt wants to walk." He paused and aimed his next words like sour spit at the old riverman's single glaring eye: "Wouldn't you like to see with two healthy eyes, Cruzatte?" Labiche said it loud enough for the whole mess to hear. He was whittling a fish hook from a burl of wood and flicked the shavings into the fire. They flared briefly and crumbled to ash. Cruzatte reacted with silent wrath, but before it could erupt, the pirate blasted: "Ever been in prison, Pierre? Ever had a man cage you, treat you like a chip of wood, like a slave?"

Now Cruzatte snarled back: "Blackie's the devil's man. Should know his place. If he don't like it, let him leave, join a tribe." He stabbed his thumb in York's direction. "He'd rather lick his fat lips at a white man's table, act like he was free."

Silence followed the outburst until Collins muttered softly: "He is free, almost, out here." The remark met with icy stares. Collins, who enjoyed making Cruzatte squirm, continued: "Clean Bratton's mess, Cruzatte, pick the worms from his food, see how you like your Christian duty. See if you could stomach what York does every day."

Cruzatte's one eye narrowed and his lips drew back.

Collins didn't care. Very few men were ready to confirm the worth of a black man beyond the price paid for his naked body on the auction block, a precious few like Drouillard, Joe Whitehouse, Labiche, John Colter, and maybe young Georgie Shannon.

Collins got up to leave and Cruzatte flicked his final comment at his back. "They should've whipped you harder, Johnny Collins."

Collins stopped, balled his fists, clenched his teeth, then kept walking. At the beginning of the journey, when he'd first signed on, he would have flung a fist in Cruzatte's rotten teeth. Today he stopped at words. To hit an old man, half his size, with one eye, proved nothing. Restraint had been a lesson hard learned. Experience and the direction of Drouillard and William Clark had redeemed him from the genial scrapper and drinker of two years ago and created a responsible member of the corps, and Collins knew he was better for it. But he could not resist flinging a final verbal dart at self-righteous Cruzatte: "Whip me and I'll gouge your good eye, old man!"

Drouillard grabbed him by the collar and pulled him out of earshot. The journey had not improved all men. Some like Hugh Hall had coarsened and their friendship cheapened. The consumption of the last whiskey this past July 4th had accelerated the decline.

Collins preferred the society of better men and chose his friends accordingly. The quiet competence of the black man attracted him. Nights, around the fire, with Labiche, Colter, and the few others, he tried to elicit conversation from the hesitant slave. At first, York spoke only in monosyllables on innocuous subjects — the weather, the river, the weight of a cask, or the heat of the fire. He sat on the smoky side of the fire, slept on the rockiest bed ground, ate the dregs that were left in the pot. He never complained and earned men's acceptance and respect, but not their friendship.

His master, William Clark, treated him as he always had. Clark would ponder the advice of pirate Labiche, half-breed Drouillard, or Frenchman Charbonneau, but invariably, because of habit long ingrained, he treated the black man like a horse or cow. Meriwether Lewis was worse and ignored him altogether. But to all other men, and to the Indian woman, Clark and Lewis were basically attentive and fair.

Collins had never owned a slave, although he knew many who had, and the treatment afforded to York irked and saddened him. He'd grown up on the western Maryland frontier, in the new settlement of Frederick, close to the former Quaker colony of Pennsylvania. To him, York was a full member of the corps, no less, no more. But to men from the tidewater and piedmont of Virginia, the newly settled lands of Kentucky, or the riverfront communities of Louisiana Territory, York was chattel. William Clark, born in Caroline County, and Meriwether Lewis, from Albemarle County, Virginia, were raised immersed in the belief. Others, too, paid as little attention to York as they did to the quantities of salmon struggling upriver.

When York walked the few yards from camp, turned his face to the heavens, and looked his God in the eye, they did not hear. When he stood at his master's side, waiting for the order to shove off, they looked straight through him. And these same men sulked like spoiled children when their own petitions went unheeded.

The corps portaged around the Columbia falls and pushed relentlessly upriver. The way was familiar, the effort prodigious, but the routine was boringly slow — row, pole, tow, and strain. Then came dinner, campfire banter, and finally rest and enveloping sleep. Up again the next morning and more of the same. The days progressed slowly, always heaving, pulling, pushing their way past the native fishermen. The moist, dense flora of the gorge gave way to clean rolling grassland that sparkled spring green in the morning sun.

Collins poled, Labiche paddled, and York, like a wheeler horse harnessed to the dugout's heavy prow, shouldered the greatest weight. He looped the rope around his chest and with the brace of his powerful spine, heaved and pulled. Labiche babbled to fill the vacant hours. Every evening, he observed: "Blackie's tired. Never gets his rest."

On April 10th, an inflowing stream stirred the river's brew to eddies of muddy brown. York stopped and stood straight to limber his back before entering the conflicting waters. It was the routine, to rest and regroup and move forward slowly where danger lurked. First the captain's dugout plumbed the depths and identified the channel. Then the others would follow in its wake, single file.

Collins drove in the pole to hold the boat steady, and waited. Labiche put up his paddle. York climbed the bank and held the tow taut while Bratton talked to calm his nerves as he always did whenever risk increased: "You two blokes want Blackie to hold back the river?" The muscular slave stood tall and erect. His broad chest rose and fell with his breathing as they watched Ordway's boat enter the meeting of waters.

Suddenly Hugh Hall, forwardmost on the tow, disappeared. Hall resurfaced, but the dugout swerved hard. The Fields brothers, paddlers, tried frantically to right the boat, but a hard wave swept it loose. It swerved backward with the current, missing York, but snagging his line. The black man sustained the first jolt with a powerful grip of massive hands. For a moment, he wavered with two boats and the river tugging his line. Collins added his strength to the pull as the Fields brothers tried in vain to disengage the errant dugout and Sergeant Ordway began to pitch heavy items into the stream. But a sudden solid wave twirled the canoe like a feather. Collins felt his grip weaken. The press of water doubled and slowly pulled York and Collins backwards. The dugout tipped, began to fill. As it capsized, Collins let go, but the harness dragged York under. Labiche grabbed his knife and with a decisive sweep cut the cord. York resurfaced, but the boat, with William Bratton trapped beneath it, began to float downstream as orders shrieked over the waters from sergeants and captains.

Collins threw down his pole and dove for Bratton. In the fish-filled water, groping for the solid feel of human flesh, he plowed through the flapping salmon. He found a face, then an arm. With his hands, Bratton had pushed aside his elk-skin cushioning, but could not kick free of the heavy hull. Collins shoved his shoulders down so as to clear the gunwales and pull the paralyzed man out from under the boat. Bratton's dead weight resisted, then broke free with a rush. Collins gained the surface, gasped air, then fell back to brace an arm under Bratton's chin and raise his head above the waves. Exhausted, he let himself drift with the flow and struck for shore several hundred yards downstream.

Drouillard and Colter rushed in to seize the ailing man while Gibson, Shannon, the Fields brothers, and hefty Sergeant Gass hauled both dugouts to shore. Collins rolled Bratton onto his stomach and lay, panting, until Drouillard came for them. Drouillard carried Bratton back upstream to where the corps was bailing the boat and setting wet cargo out to dry. Miraculously the only loss was two bushels of diluted salt.

Next day they began again, Collins with knees so cramped that he wondered if he would ever again be able stand erect, walk, or ride a horse. He was beginning to detest the river and to envy Bratton who never had to exert physical effort. He yearned to lie still like Bratton and extend his six-foot frame its full length for hours at a time and to give his eyes relief from the water's glassy sheen. When at last they beached amid another horde of natives, he hobbled to shore and collapsed into his blankets without dinner.

Late in the night, before the fire died, he felt a hand squeeze his shoulder. It was York with meat and boiled

Indian cous and he whispered: "Massa Clark an' Mister Drouillard says I should watch while you eat."

Collins forced down the meal, but the cous wadded like an undigested cud in his stomach and cancelled all efforts to sleep. He listened to the restless snores of other men and the endless clatter of native activity. Night and day their activity never stopped. It blended unintelligibly with the babblings of the corps, the names of distant mothers and sweethearts and memories of home and hearth. Whitehouse, who rested near Collins and could read, ranted incoherently about a king who valued a horse more than his kingdom. Some thought him mad but Collins deemed him exactly right, and, when finally he fell to snoring, he dreamed of horses.

Of all the men who slept, only the slave was silent. The man who could not admit desire or entertain ambition, the man who portrayed submission in every bend of back and bow of head, the man to whom many would deny his very manhood, slept more soundly than all the rest.

April 12th, dawn light crept slowly over the lip of hills. York was up, the sounds of his prayer echoing softly. John Colter was wadding dry grass into clumps for kindling to start the fire because no trees grew nearby and the Indians had picked the river clean of driftwood. George Shannon held a blanket to shield the budding embers from the wind. No one had bothered to awaken Collins. He rolled, stood up, and moved instinctively toward the warmth.

116

Shannon smiled up at him and flipped a casual remark: "Saw a horse this mornin', first decent one on the river."

John Colter laughed sarcastically. "And I saw the gates o' heaven openin'. You're dreamin', boy. Horses are scarce as trees here, where grass won't even grow."

Collins laughed, too. "No horses here, no grass feed, just rocks an' mud." He inquired: "How's Bratt?"

"Sleepin' all day, he rails all night, but he's tough, he survived." Shannon paused, stared at Collins, then resumed: "An Indian was leadin' a fat nag like you rode over the mountains, Johnny, loaded all over with nets an' baskets, nose an' tail pokin' out like pins in a cushion. I told the sergeant."

Colter's wadded grass flamed softly and he looked up. "Might be ridin', next week, back to your Mandan bride, an' on home to Saint Louie, eh, Johnny?"

They finished breakfast and took up positions, slapping aside the sex-starved fish, towing, arm over arm, step by slow step, around fish-filled weirs and over straining nets. All day long, to distract himself from the grueling effort, John Collins imagined horses he'd known: sway-backed Dolly who had taught the Collins boys to ride, the bay that was his when he'd signed on, and the hefty Indian ponies that he'd offered in dowry to the father of Laughing Water. Thoughts of horses, like faithful friends, brought him assurance and hope, but even they could never dispel the dream of Laughing Water.

On April 14th, he stood in the stern manning the long pole. With each press forward, he tugged the pole from the alluvial mud and pushed it down again a few feet farther upriver. Labiche and York towed. They passed more villages of many lodges. Indians crammed the shores in ever greater numbers. That night, they barely allowed the corps space to moor and camp.

"Worse than Spaniards with their greed, worse than Saint Louis traders," Labiche babbled as they shoved the dugout up onto the beach for the night.

A slap and a hard jerk whirled Collins around as a skinny urchin pulled at the sling that held his rifle. A boy, a youth of four or five years, not taller than his waist, pitched the weapon to a leggy man who caught it on the fly and raced away. Collins grabbed the boy, handed him to John Colter, and pursued. But the crowd of Indians pressed him back.

Drouillard was closer, swung his knife, and charged after the thief. He caught the man by the hair, jerked the gun away, and smacked him hard in the chest with the butt, then passed the gun to Collins and the boy to Sergeant Gass.

Gass drew his tomahawk and raised it like a sword of judgment over the boy's head. His Irish voice blasted outrage: "Another urchin thief!"

Two shrieking women rushed forward. Collins and Drouillard lay hold of them both as Charbonneau's wife appeared with her own babe strapped to her back. Charbonneau plodded heavily after, shouting: "He is but a child! You would not kill my Baptiste, my Pomp!"

Gass lowered the blade, but he chopped off a lock of black hair and handed it to the mother with an admonition: "Be ye witch or loving mother, ye coddle a bloody thief." With a scowl, he whirled on his heel and met Drouillard's fiery glare. "A curse on all o' the heathens who teach their wee ones to thieve and pillage."

The boy fled into the angry mass and Drouillard pronounced with icy calm: "Time for us all to get off this river."

CHAPTER
TEN

By April 19th, the expedition had spotted the towering mountains ahead. John Collins tossed under his thin covering of patched skins and listened to the west wind howl. No one slept soundly except York who lay silently and motionlessly, and always awakened refreshed. He marched off to say his prayers while the rest of the corps huddled sullenly around the fire and munched their meager breakfast.

The river was running fast, and the order to shove off did not come. Impatience as always wore on both officers and men. Collins and Labiche sat with the rest of the corps near the boats on the shore. Cruzatte fiddled; the squeaky music and wagging tongues filled idle, anxious minutes.

The waiting irritated Bratton more than most and he grew increasingly critical. "You got no cause to fiddle, Cruzatte? Sounds like a cat in water. You supposed to pilot the boats an' you almost drowned me." Cruzatte who had conducted the canoes through many a dangerous rapid kept fiddling. Lately he was fiddling more, reveling in the pleasures of sound, not sight, because his one eye was failing.

"What's an old riverman to do, stare at his own nose?" Colter said, adding with a crude chuckle: "Let 'im fiddle for 'is supper." In answering Bratton, Colter only irritated Cruzatte.

Cruzatte dropped the instrument and pointed a bony finger at Colter. "Old I ain't, an' I can see sure as Drouillard can watch a worm wiggle. It's Labiche an' Collins an' the blackie, an' you, John Colter, dreamin' o' whiskey an' women an' your glitterin' gold when you should've been watchin' the river. It's you an' Collins let the boat flip."

Collins tensed visibly, but Drouillard's tight grip on his biceps stopped him. "Words counter words, Johnny, not fists and kicks." It was an unwritten rule on the expedition that speech alone never provoked open rebuke, and that punishment was for actions only.

But words could inflame, and Labiche answered insult for insult. "You couldn't sight a cloud in a bare blue sky, Cruzatte." Labiche was close to the truth and added: "If your eye's fogging, tell us, old man. Dangerous not to."

Cruzatte rubbed the patch that covered his empty socket. "Don't need two eyes. I can feel how water flows. Spent my whole life feelin' rivers."

"Feel water like you feel a big titty, eh, Frenchie?" Sergeant Gass meant to ease the dispute and he laughed when he said it, but he offended Cruzatte's strict rectitude.

The old man's spine snapped stiff and his jaw set, but the creases in his face were etched more by fear than anger. Cruzatte was wasting like Bratton, concealing weakness, replacing dwindling sight with prickly speech. He usually chose his targets carefully, men like Bratton, who would not fight back, and the black slave. Now warily he retracted his assault on Collins and Labiche: "Maybe it was Blackie liked to have drowned us all. Maybe he's the ghost that's stealin' us blind. Never could see a blackie in the dark."

Collins peered at York's stoic face and drooping eyelids and changed the subject. He said — "Storm's brewin'." — but the sun was shining.

The river calmed and they fought their way fifteen miles upstream that day to the base of boiling rapids where they came ashore early and camped high on an open slope. A few ragged lodges, homes to the poorest Indians, hemmed the river below them. The west wind fanned the flames of the fire. They ate a fat buck that Drouillard had killed and watched the Indians cook their fishy meal in the village below. The odor rose on an updraft and Collins rubbed his nose. With a stick, he poked aimlessly at the fire. Suddenly he raised his skinny stick toward an Indian scaffold draped with strips of pink salmon and exclaimed: "Four hoofs and a tail or my eyes are seein' visions!"

Huge, tottering packs obscured all but the head, lower legs, hoofs, and tail of a horse. Collins jumped up, ready to hurtle down the hill after the beast, but Drouillard stopped him short. He grabbed Collins's knife, the pirate's blade with inlaid stone that Labiche had given him and that he kept secreted, strapped tightly against his thigh. Drouillard held it by its blade and waved the handle temptingly. When Collins reached to snatch it back, Drouillard whipped it out of reach, saying: "This is why they can steal with impunity. Mind it more carefully or you will lose it to a craftier thief than I." Again he directed the hilt toward Collins, who wrapped his palm around the blue gemstone in the handle and returned the knife to its sheath.

Meriwether Lewis had spotted the horse, too. Lewis was sitting by his own small fire, munching mechanically, when he interrupted his dinner to summon Drouillard. Drouillard came, sat, and Lewis pointed a finger at the forlorn animal. "Tomorrow, see if there are more and ask if they will sell."

"You mean trade?" Lewis refused to admit how little was left to trade, and Drouillard flung the question insolently back in his face. But in the morning, he went and returned with the surly owner, a man of the Enesher nation, whose beady eyes receded beneath a thick curtain of black bangs. A stream of incomprehensible syllables whistled from spaces between the man's teeth. The price of a horse was high. The man's face spread in a toothy grin and he blared: *"Fusées."* Lewis repeated: "Guns." And Drouillard explained: "He has no interest in knives, not even Collins's jeweled dagger, and he has another fat horse for you to eat, sir."

Lewis rose to address the man. "How many guns?"

The Indian raised a fist, extended his thumb, index, and middle fingers, and declared: "Canoe, three. Gun, two." He spoke broken English and had traded before with the ships' people.

"We have no canoes to spare." Lewis, who could anger quickly at the incompetence of Collins or Hall, contained his wrath at this overt native perversity, but Drouillard, who usually evinced no emotion, let his outrage erupt and accosted the man: "A price we cannot pay. What for guns? To shoot your enemies? To shoot us?" The loud comment passed quickly through the corps with a tug of sleeve or a jab of elbow. No man doubted the thieving Eneshers would also kill if they sensed an advantage.

Drouillard calmed himself muttering: "The guns provide our meat. They are our only assurance of safety and life. Ahead, upriver, where the grass grows thick, there will be fitter, stronger animals."

With enforced calm, Lewis questioned the Indian: "How far to the horse people's villages?" The man blabbered incomprehensible syllables until Drouillard seized him by the throat. Only then did he confess: "One long day's walk, by horse." A murderous shadow passed from Lewis's ruddy face as he waved a dismissive hand: "Away with the blackguard. Get me Captain Clark." Clark had elected to dine at the central fire in company of his men.

Darkness was falling when Clark, who had been hunting all day, came, with Drouillard, to confront Lewis who stood brooding, facing the purpling night with his back to the flames of the fire and the red setting sun. Captain Lewis's thin frame cast a long shadow and his shrill voice carried easily to the huddle of enlisted men: "We cannot remain on this river, Will. Rain, theft, the natives who feign friendship, then betray us, are still with us." He paused, then continued and his voice rose in a wild crescendo: "They watch, like evil stars behind clouds of night. We cannot see them and we have no power to resist them!" He whirled on his heel and settled a fierce gaze on the tall silhouette of Georges Drouillard. "Mister Drouillard, choose good men. Go to these villages one day's walk away on the plateau where pastures are blooming, and find us horses enough to reach the good Nez Percé." Lewis's voice echoed loudly for all to hear. He did not say *trade* or *buy*. Collins caught the omission. Drouillard was as free to steal as the light-fingered natives.

William Clark raised a lingering doubt: "We have no proof they have animals, Meri. Drouillard goes on foot. In a conflict, horsemen will have a clear advantage."

Lewis had a ready answer. "Mister Drouillard is a resourceful man," he snapped, and left execution and outcome to Captain Clark.

The men resumed guarded chatter as William Clark sought out Privates Colter and Collins. "You two who have eyes for a good horse, go with Drouillard. Choose strong, docile animals. Drive them here and you will have redeemed your good name in Captain Lewis's eyes."

Collins mumbled audibly: "Is that possible, sir?"

Clark ignored the outburst. He turned to go and came face to face with Lewis who stood with arms folded stubbornly across his chest, behind him.

With nervous fingertips, Lewis drummed his elbows as he proclaimed: "And, Will, you will lead a party to the Skilloots, to learn if they, too, have animals."

Clark's jaw dropped. The Skilloots were known murderers who had nearly killed Private Hugh McNeal on the way west.

Meriwether Lewis continued talking as if to convince himself that the missions to which he had just assigned his two best leaders posed no threat. He declared loudly: "These Indians do not kill and we must not kill them." He returned to his private fire, sat, placed his hands firmly on his knees, sucked in air, and repeated to himself what his best rivermen, Labiche and Cruzatte, had been telling him for days: "The dugouts are not fit to brave the river farther. The wood is soft as a sponge. In a few days, they'll sink from our own weight." He sat alone and no one was there to hear, because he slept with Charbonneau, the woman, and the babe who were already asleep. Clark and the sergeants chose to bed with the corps. Firelight danced across the deep furrows of Lewis's face as he concluded: "Overland, we shall evade pursuit and escape the river's gremlins." Satisfied, he nodded, settled into his bedding, and slept.

After the captains had both fallen asleep, John Colter remarked to Collins: "Lewie's dreamin'. Where's the Injun that'll let you an' me steal his horse without a fight?" He kicked a dead coal back into the fire. It flamed brightly and he grumbled: "He don' like us much . . . don't like Clark neither, handin' 'im a job to get ourselves killed. Clark wouldn't give it to a slave."

Cynically Collins replied: "We'll have to steal the fastest horse."

Drouillard, Collins, Labiche, and John Colter remained by the fire as the night shadows lengthened. When Labiche got up to leave, Drouillard murmured: "You come too, pirate, to buy horses. The natives are afraid of you."

But Collins objected. "Labiche rides like a flappin' fowl. If they pursue, he can only slow the chase." François Labiche, pirate and gambler, could maneuver a canoe through boiling rapids and cheat the wiliest native at a game, but he couldn't steer a horse.

Drouillard nodded. "We need another man. Let Georgie Shannon come. Wake him. Tell him to assemble at the square rock one hour before dawn."

Blood-red stripes scratched the dawn sky when the sounds of early morning rattled Collins's dreams. He looked around. Matted grass marked the spaces where Clark's men had slept. They had left earlier. When Drouillard came to rouse him, he kicked George Shannon awake and they dressed, slung sacks and rifles over their shoulders, and scrambled to the square rock.

Drouillard and Colter were already there. Colter observed: "River's running high. Eat now. Wait for full light to cross." He passed around charred chunks of meat, leftovers from the night before. The lean meat didn't begin to satisfy hunger. Collins was still chewing as they headed for the boats. He washed the tasteless bites down with water as they crossed silently to the southern shore and moved east over dry, open grassland. The expanse looked strangely familiar, like the prairie of the central plains that surrounded

Matootonha village of the Mandans, but there were no buffalo, no round earth lodges where friendly Mandans welcomed and Laughing Water waited. Collins felt his heart constrict when he thought of her as if a vise were closing inexorably around his chest. He thought of her too often.

John Colter harbored no such distraction. He was ebullient. "Horses, Johnny, are man's companions and helpers. I can feel my backside slappin' a saddle, wind in my hair, gallopin' across the prairie all the way back to my strike." He meant the few gold nuggets that he had scratched from the bank of a creek somewhere in the tallest mountains.

His enthusiasm met with Collins's mockery: "What strike? Stop dreamin', Colt. With no saddle on these skinny runts, it'll be like ridin' a split rail."

Shannon added: "Lucky if we can walk 'em home." He stopped because Drouillard had stopped ahead of him.

Drouillard was staring straight ahead and called: "Riders coming up the trail! Load your rifles!"

The four men paired back to back, primed and cocked their rifles.

The horses were tightly grouped and ridden by six burly Indians. They galloped up and came to a jarring, stiff-legged halt in a cloud of dust on both sides of the waiting men. Suddenly Drouillard put up his gun and bellowed: "Guns up! No shooting, boys!"

The newcomers were Cayuses who listened to the offer to trade and conducted the party to a green valley where their herds grazed on the fresh spring growth.

Collins counted 200 fit, serviceable animals. The four bedded that night within cheerful sight of the herd, but they slept fitfully and took turns watching with loaded rifles.

In the morning, bargaining began. The Indians agreed to trade three sway-backed mares, then cancelled the bargain. Drouillard gave a knife for a gimpy, head-bobbing bay that Collins immediately pronounced lame. "Can't carry hisself. How's he gonna carry Bratt?"

An old, crippled Indian, leaning on a crutch, stood with the horse as Drouillard continued: "Relief from his pains is all he asks. It's a price we can pay." He took the horse and started back to camp. The Indian followed. He was still trundling along behind when they arrived in camp.

Lewis wrinkled his nose at the sight of him. "A cripple with a bedraggled animal whose leg is bowed, with open sores where we would place our packs?"

Drouillard explained: "If we cure this man, they may find us more."

A red flash of anger crossed Lewis's brow as he settled his glance on Collins, not Drouillard. "Was this your doing, Private? The man is sick as Bratton, who I cannot cure, and the horse is lame. Nomadic peoples would have left them both behind to die." His teeth snapped shut. With a flick of wrist, he dismissed Collins: "Away with you and your imbecile designs. Do with them as you please, but keep them out of my sight." He turned on Drouillard, screeching: "You think I can make Lazarus rise from the dead? The horse is fit

129

to eat, not ride! And the man smells of urine and sweat." He clamped his mouth shut, closed his eyes, inhaled, and balled his trembling fingers into tight fists, muttering: "Tell York to clean him up and lay him with Bratton near the fire. And see what you can make of the nag."

When he turned away, Drouillard spoke to Pryor: "The man says he owns many horses, that his son will bring more for us to inspect."

Pryor assented with a single word: "Good."

Drouillard passed a hat dutifully from man to man, begging buttons, buckles, anything that could be traded for a horse. The pickings were lean. Clark persuaded Lewis to pitch in his lace-trimmed coat, lamenting: "More than twice what we offered the Shoshones for one horse."

Indians came, looked, fingered the frilled collar and cuffs and assorted buttons, and walked away.

Finally Pryor braved Lewis's wrath: "They want guns, sir, not beads, and the old man wants a cure."

Lewis did not respond. His shoulders rounded and he seemed to shrink. Only the stiff barrel of his rifle held him upright as he murmured: "They think me a miracle worker. What will be the consequence if I fail to cure him?"

"We have no other choice, sir?"

"Then take me to the stinking man."

York had done well. The man was clean, his hair combed. Lewis wrapped the spindly legs in hot wet blankets and directed the slave. "Keep them as hot as he can stand. Do the same for Bratton."

Light was fading when the man's son appeared with two more animals: a stunted gelding, short-legged and hard-gaited, fit only to pack gear, and a paint mare with a white eye, whose head hung, nose to ground, like a pendulum. Drouillard intercepted them, stroked the mare's ewed neck, turned suddenly, and bellowed across the camp: "Johnny, come see if you know this horse!"

Collins recognized the ice-blue eye immediately, even from a distance. "She's the same one Labiche rode over the mountains, the mare with the foal we killed and ate." He came and ran a hand down the foreleg to the ankle, and his fingers came away sticky with pus. "A good soaking . . . a salt plaster to draw out the foulness." He bridled suddenly and snapped erect as Meriwether Lewis approached.

Lewis looked down his length of nose. "Another horse, another cripple, Private, for me to redeem?"

"With your permission, sir, I will be responsible for her care." When Lewis didn't answer, Collins led the mare away.

The following day, William Clark returned to camp empty-handed. Grimly Lewis wrung his hands and watched Clark's party straggle in. Seaman, his black retriever, set his head on his master's knee and Meriwether Lewis uncrimped his fingers to caress the broad black head. But when he went with Clark to inspect the horse, he expressed no pity for the animal. "In three days, Will, that mare must carry Bratton or we shoot her for meat."

Clark did not contest. A vein in his cheek throbbed wildly and he rubbed it to mask his anxiety, then he declared softly: "I'll see to the mare and Collins myself, Meri."

Collins held the horse while Clark pierced the pustule and directed: "Stand her in the river, Private, to cleanse the wound."

Collins picketed the mare knee-high in the river and made his bed nearby on the bank. In the morning, when the breeze blew lightly out of the west and York called on his God, the crippled Indian walked and Collins brought the mare to Captain Clark. The ankle was still swollen, but the mare plodded soundly, and Collins declared: "She's ready, sir. She'll carry Bratt."

The Indian was true to his word. At noon, Drouillard arrived leading another horse, a sorrel stud, sleek and alert as a thoroughbred racer. He reported to Clark before Lewis could protest. "The sick man who you cured was even more grateful, sir."

John Colter rubbed his hairy chin and poked Collins hard in the ribs. "That red one's Spanish or Brit bred, Johnny, hot-blooded. They think we'll break our scrawny necks tryin' to ride her."

Collins rose to the challenge, licked his lip, and quipped: "I can't wait to try."

CHAPTER
ELEVEN

Ochoa remained on his giant canoe at the foot of the falls, anchored on the soft waves of a quiet backwater. He took his place daily on the platform in the bow beside his twelve-pounder, behind the huge raven's beak. Parrish had fashioned a high-backed chair with thick cushions of the pelts of the sea otter. From his perch, Ochoa surveyed shore and ship and held sway over the river natives.

Although the Indians had assigned a comfortable lodge for sleeping and eating, Ochoa was not comfortable on land and preferred his water-borne home. His fealty to England had receded as his prestige among the river tribes increased.

But Douglas grew restless. He was a thin, callow youth. He had a knobby head, ruddy complexion, and pale blond hair that streaked like spun gold in the west wind. His build and coloring contrasted starkly with the shorter, darker natives so that the women, who came to him nightly, called him Pale Devil, thought him ugly, and peered at him suspiciously from slitted eyes. He considered their flat faces deformed and reacted to their suspicions with anger and brutality. His contempt for the native peoples and for the misguided men who had led him into this wasteland subsided only when he consumed rum in ever greater quantities. But rum inflamed a violent temper that let loose its fury on the native population. On a drunken rampage, Douglas had already outraged one chief, a Chinook, when he struck the chief's daughter, broke her nose, and ruined the girl's flat profile forever. The father had dragged his maimed daughter to Ochoa who placated him with the gift of a musket, and confined Douglas to the belly of the *Devil's Bird* for one day. Released, Douglas resumed his old habits with renewed zeal.

The month was April and Ochoa vowed to be rid of the troublemaker for good. He summoned Parrish, an intelligent man who grasped instinctively both Markham's and Ochoa's motives. Parrish had been forced into a life on the sea when an impressment gang seized him. But he had been apprenticed to a carpenter, knew the grains and density of woods, and could cut a perfect mortise and tenon. He had determined immediately that the *Phoenix*'s timbers were in need of repair. Shipworms had attacked the ship. Now on the western shores of the Americas, the hull had become so riddled with worm and penetrated with water that he'd kept pumps almost constantly running. Markham never went below decks and never noticed that shipworms were chewing their way through the thick planking. The HMS *Phoenix* could never brace the mighty Pacific winds and waters. So, glad to escape the *Phoenix*'s fate, Parrish had followed Ochoa willingly and spent the winter scheming his own future, wandering the riverbanks, squirreling away furs, concealing them carefully in neat bundles at intervals along the river.

Ochoa sought the collusion of Parrish in sealing Douglas's fate. He invited them both to dine and motioned them to soft cushions of thick otter in the belly of the boat, away from the prying eyes of the natives. A woman served jugs of fine Barbadian rum. Ochoa opened the discourse with a casual nod and *pop* of cork and passed the jug. "Drink gentlemen. It's from the best of Markham's store. I stole it myself."

Parrish met Ochoa's steady gaze with a genial nod and wrapped his bony fingers around the jug. He touched it to his lips, but did not sip. Douglas encircled the rim with his mouth and let the liquid glide liberally down his throat. Ochoa watched the knot in his goose's neck throb every time he swallowed. The man would drink himself to a watery grave.

After Parrish sipped a second time, Ochoa raised his glass to announce the purpose of the interview. He ignored Douglas and addressed his remarks to Parrish: "To future alternatives, Mister Parrish." He sipped and smacked his lips. "The Americans are on their way east. Our scouts tell me the land beyond the river, where they are headed, is barren." He caught a white glimmer in Parrish's narrowed eye and a twist of greedy lip. Avarice was a predictable sin, but encasing Parrish in an acquisitive web would require patience and subtlety. He continued: "Mister Parrish, you and I can pursue the Americans, grab their few firearms and some powder, but we would risk loss of this boat and the devotion of these fine Chinooks." He did not mention the many bales of furs that Parrish had amassed, and conjectured simply: "Or we can remain here and enrich ourselves when the trading ships return."

Parrish, a spidery, long-limbed man, sensed precisely what Ochoa intended, but concealed his intentions behind the hardened lines and frozen muscles of an expressionless face. He said nothing. Douglas grinned stupidly and took another swig.

Ochoa continued in a voice oily with flattery: "Aboard the *Phoenix*, you were an able servant, Mister Parrish, deserving of promotion and reward, recognition that was denied to you. You were a seaman who could never aspire to rank or title. Here on the river, you command respect, even awe." He paused for emphasis. "You enjoy more comfort than ever before in your life."

The empty jug crashed to the floor and rolled against the planks. Douglas had sucked it dry and blabbered incoherently: "Beg pardon, sir, Parrish gi' me furs. Never gimme rum." He shot a fawning glance at Ochoa who made no attempt to open a second jug.

Parrish had not blinked. His eyes darted everywhere, measuring Ochoa while Ochoa scrutinized him. An interval of silence elapsed while Parrish judged carefully what he would say. He chose words like ripened fruits and they slipped sweetly off his tongue. He observed: "There's a king's riches in furs."

Ochoa waited for Douglas to collapse before he smiled and said: "Return to the *Phoenix* and Markham will requisition any furs we've amassed and claim the proceeds for himself. If we refuse him, he'll confine us to quarters, whip or throw us to the sharks. You and I know the furs will end up on the ocean's floor. The fruits of our labors, Mister Parrish, have far greater value." Parrish's tongue moved across his teeth as Ochoa pressed his argument: "We will find other ships, Spanish, Russian, or American, and trade furs for rum or whatever else will ease our lives and lure these natives to serve us well."

Parrish raised a brow at Ochoa's deviousness. Still he did not commit to any action, but acceded agreeably. "A fair life here on the river would not be unpleasant, if the Brits don't hang us for mutineers."

"We will have saved ourselves from a foundering ship and tried to survive like any worthy seaman," Ochoa continued. "We would be castaways, lucky to have escaped with our lives. They will raise no charges against us, prescribe no punishment. Whalers, China traders, Russians, Spanish sloops, all ply these waters as well as His Majesty's ships and we will trade with any or all of these." Ochoa paused again, then pressed his argument: "You are the carpenter, Mister Parrish. You know the condition of the *Phoenix*'s timbers. Stiles also knew. It did not surprise me that he volunteered to come with us." He paused. "Poor Stiles . . . vanished in the wilderness." He raised his glass. "I miss him and drink to his fond memory." He sipped and sat back. "As for mutiny, our mission is legitimate. I have Markham's letter and his official seal." Finally Ochoa aimed his final question well. "Can I depend on your co-operation and support, Mister Parrish?"

Parrish's pinched face broke into a wide grin. "Aye, Ochoa. I'm with you." But he would not address the man as sir.

"Then we drink to seal our pact." Ochoa uncorked a second jug and poured out two cups. He waited while Parrish drank, set it down, and cast a dismissive glance at Douglas who lay, spread-eagled, on the floor. "He'll go willingly back to the *Phoenix* when I deny him rum." He swiped a sleeve across his wet lips.

They talked on. Ochoa had developed plans and explained carefully: "The American fort, on the River Netul, near the Clatsop villages, is well back from the sea, hidden from the prying eyes of a ship's look-out. It will serve well as our post. The Clatsops will not trouble us. They are too weak to resist the Chinooks and will welcome us. And we will enrich them, too."

Parrish was grinning broadly now: "I drink to ye, Ochoa. You're a smart man." He grabbed the jug, threw his head back, and swallowed long and hard. Then he licked the drops from the rim of the jug. "'Tis good rum. A pity that Markham's barrels will sink with the *Phoenix*, but, I take it, you've hauled most of them here." He smiled and met Ochoa's gaze. Their eyes locked in a beam of agreement. Abruptly Parrish stood up. The interview was at an end.

Ochoa watched him go, then dragged Douglas out across the gangplank to dry land and left him there.

Darkness was falling. Ochoa retired to the comfortable lodge the Chinooks had erected for him. A woman was waiting. She lay at his side and he took her quickly with brutish passion and sent her away. Parrish was already asleep when Ochoa stretched lengthwise on his bed. Without the lap of water and sway of boat, he could not sleep. He counted the myriad stars poking through the smoke hole, watched clouds blow in and smear what light there was. Smoke from the fire compounded the gloom as his active mind dispelled the shadows and he contemplated Markham's doom. The foolish captain would set sail soon for the Sandwich Islands. Perhaps he already had. Gleefully Ochoa willed Markham's total destruction, and fell asleep.

In the morning, he resumed his high seat in the *Devil's Bird* and summoned Douglas, who tripped over the canoe's interior struts and fell, face first, at Ochoa's feet. A trickle of blood seeped from the corner of his mouth. He let it drip and muttered: "You called, sir."

Ochoa smiled, but the man disgusted more than pleased him. He began: "Mister Douglas, you've drunk the dregs and we have no further rum to ease your troubles. The month is April and the *Phoenix* will anchor again shortly in the estuary. I thought you, who are so fond of spirits, most able and willing to fetch us more from Captain Markham's stores." He paused, smiled graciously, and continued:

"And, of course, you will report news of our success to Captain Markham. I will prepare a dispatch."

Douglas blinked and blurted: "Aye, sir. Pleasure, sir." The words were slurred. He could not complete his thought.

"Take a sturdy canoe and a Chinook guide. Go downriver, the way we have come. Mister Parrish will start you on your way. Float with the current. It's an easy trip. Start at sunup."

Douglas slept late. Well after sunup, he meandered to the river. An Indian helped him climb into the canoe. The dispatch was a blank scroll, rolled and carefully sealed with wax that Parrish delivered to Douglas as he was about to shove off. Parrish agreeably offered to accompany them for the first mile. The canoe was old but sturdy enough for the three paddlers to go a short distance. They sailed smoothly downriver to the place where salt water met fresh and the waters mixed and eddied. The tide was coming in, rushing up on a gentle bore as the river flowed down. Douglas was slouched in the bow when the canoe hit. He braced the force and plunged in his paddle to send the boat through the wave. At the same instant, Parrish and the Indian drove their paddles backward. The boat's sudden lurch threw Douglas's weight forward. He felt the knife stab the soft of his back, but he barely felt the push, gave a short moan, and slipped over the side. The pain was great. He breathed in to ease it and fluid filled his lungs. He opened his mouth to cry out, but the river rushed in and smothered his cry. He came to the surface once, saw the canoe pulling away, closed his eyes, and sank beneath the water.

Parrish had never left his seat. He still held his knife and washed the blood from the blade in the river. Then he and the Indian paddled to shore. He felt no remorse. Rigging a sail required a quick eye and steady hand. Douglas had neither. And trapping fur animals in the rivers required stamina and intelligence that he also lacked. Douglas would have died anyway in a ship's service, fallen from off the ship's high spars to the hard deck below, or in the endless forests, like Stiles, he would have made easy prey.

Downstream, Parrish went ashore. He dismissed the Chinook, who accepted the canoe for his service and continued downriver to his village. Parrish trudged an easy mile back upriver, checking his trap lines and whistling to himself as he went, and arrived at the *Devil's Bird* before nightfall.

Two days later, a fisherman, another Indian, pulled a bloated body from the mouth of his weir. When he spotted Douglas's silver-blond hair, he cursed. He lugged the body by its long pale hair off the weir, pushed it into the fast current, and watched it float away toward the estuary and the endless ocean beyond. Then he waited to trap his next fish.

Ochoa welcomed Parrish on his return. Parrish's report was brief. "The man is dead. Drink and the river 'ave washed him away." They celebrated with another jug each of good Barbadian rum.

Finally Ochoa put down his drink and questioned: "Now, Mister Parrish, should we bother ourselves with American booty?"

Parrish had drunk only sparingly and answered with the discretion of a seasoned diplomat. "They've guns, sir. That's all. They can't go far."

Neither man realized that horses would spirit the Americans swiftly on their way. Neither man had ever ridden a horse.

CHAPTER
TWELVE

Four horses were not enough for the corps now that they were moving to higher, cooler climes, toward lofty mountains still distant but looming. Collins had awakened abruptly, shivering from cold, in the early dawn. The month of April waned and the weather was cool. On April 26th, when Collins awakened, a light film of snow blanketed the ground. His covering of skins were wet and lay heavy and chill across his chest. The wind whistled over the bare campground and the only sound that shook his sleep-dulled brain was the steady munch of the red horse picketed nearby. Collins threw back his cover, sat up, and brushed away the coating of wet snow. At the same time, the horse threw up his head and pricked his ears and Drouillard rolled silently into the shadows.

The steady plod of another horse barely scuffed the new-fallen snow. Collins blinked as the hazy silhouette of a horse and rider gradually emerged from the dimness. He knew from the easy slouch with which he sat the horse the rider was Indian. He felt for the pirate's dagger that lay cold against the skin of his thigh. When flints were wet and a rifle's pan covered with ice, the knife was his only sure defense. Where were the guards? Had they fallen asleep, failed to alert the camp?

Collins called out, and Indian and horse froze. Sleepy men blinked awake, groped for weapons, and squinted into the haze. Labiche stood up, half awake, half naked, and Collins pulled him down. "You make a target of yourself."

Trying to maintain some semblance of decorum, Captain Lewis shoved his arms into his uniform coat, shouting: "Hold your fire!" Sergeant Gass ignited a torch of dried grasses, which burst instantly into bright flame and consumed its fuel rapidly.

The flame illuminated the Indian's face long enough for Gass to exclaim: "By the dam that bred me, 'tis a friendly bone in the nose! Georgie Shannon, stoke the fire."

The torch shed a diminishing circle of light. The newcomer moved into its broad halo and stopped for all to see. He was a man of medium height. He did not resemble the pie-faced thieves of the Columbia basin who had driven Captain Lewis to crazed distraction. He had a full mouth, sharp, hooked nose whose cartilage was pierced by a thin stick of white bone, heavy brow, and intelligent, inquisitive, brown eyes. His hair that he wore in plaits wrapped in white skins, accentuated the bony angles of his face. A striped blanket, held by a wide sash around his middle, enveloped his shoulders to keep out the chill. His horse was a big-barreled, short-legged dun with a splash of speckled white over the rump. It matched the Indian's own thickly muscled physique.

Gass's light went out and he shouted: "Another torch, my boys, and stir the fire so we can welcome our distinguished guest!"

John Colter, who had braided handfuls of grass to start the fire, wrapped one around a pole and held it high.

With a twist of wrist and invisible touch of leg, the Indian wheeled his animal to face Gass who had done most of the talking. In a graceful, fluid motion, he dismounted and advanced toward Colter's light. A light wind lifted the braid that covered his left ear and ran along his neck, over his collar bone, down half the length of his chest. For a moment the light of the torch revealed the skin beneath that was puckered and red. Labiche saw it and observed audibly to Collins: "A cutlass struck that mark." The braid settled back in its place when the wind died, and the Indian turned his head at the sound of the pirate's voice.

Colter's light was also burning down and the man moved toward the fire to see more clearly. Uncertain who was leader, he settled his gaze on tall, dark Drouillard and slowly made his intentions known.

Drouillard interpreted his motions and what words he could decipher in a loud voice for the entire camp to hear. "He claims he has horses pastured somewhere above the river. He lent them to the river tribes during the fall salmon run in exchange for a percentage of the harvest. He has come to collect payment and drive the horses back to the high pastures of his people where they will fatten on the rich mountain grasses before carrying his people over the mountains to hunt the

144

buffalo. His helpers have sickened from the rotting disease that the ships bring and he is only one man. He is sad because he has lost his friends, and he is tired. The beasts are too many and he asks our help. He remembers the white men who came like ghosts of men out of the mountains and who regained their life and strength with his people. He asks if we are those same men."

Drouillard answered: "Aye, we are they."

Nodding, Meriwether Lewis came up beside him. Drouillard stepped back. Lewis raised an open hand in friendship and repeated: "We are those same. Tell him."

Horse and man pivoted again agilely to face Lewis.

Drouillard continued: "He begs our help in herding his horses. He asks that we allow him to warm himself by our fire and rest his tired horse." Drouillard added cautiously: "He does not look like a man who begs."

"How many horses? Where are they?" Lewis pressed for details as news of horses blew like a lively spark over the camp. If the captains could strike a bargain, they could all mount and ride.

Impatiently Lewis flashed his hands with the fingers spread wide. "We need many horses, five times the fingers on both my hands." He snapped impatiently: "Tell him. Tell him!"

Clark marched up beside Lewis as Drouillard continued to interpret. "He has lost men and needs help collecting the animals. In return, he will give each of five men, who helps, a mount. And he will guide us to his people."

The entire corps broke into a wild cheer. Men rallied to help.

As soon as the sun burned off the dawn's haze, Colter, Collins, Shannon, Warner, and Joe Fields followed the Indian into the grassy hills. They gathered over forty animals and drove them into camp. By noon, with the four horses already obtained, there was transport for everyone.

But the animals were unruly and wild, overworked and underfed by the river tribes during the fall salmon run, then turned loose to wander and feed on the lush grasses of the plateau. Now they were healthy and fit and too used to freedom. Most had not seen a human in months. Herded together, they refused to settle. Saddled and packed, they laid their ears back, nipped, and kicked.

To each man, Clark assigned a mount. Collins drew the fiery red stallion over the objections of Meriwether Lewis and pleas of John Colter who drew a leggy black. Labiche would ride the gentle, blue-eyed mare. They found a soft-gaited gray for Bratton and lashed his useless legs to a makeshift saddle. They loaded supplies for thirty men. Captain Clark called a final roll and they mounted.

The Indian led. Colter, Collins, Shannon, and Joe Whitehouse rode with the herd. The captains rode behind, then Charbonneau, his wife, and Drouillard, his keen eyes scouting each crease of rock for enemies and game. The men with pack horses followed. Finally, at the end, York, on a shaggy runt, led Bratton who flapped like a fresh kill over the gray's stubby neck.

The Indian set a rapid pace inland past giant slabs of basalt, over hard, resistant rock, along a creek where generations of native feet had worn the earth to a slippery veneer. Grass sprouted spring-green in irregular clumps along the creekbank. Cottonwood, elder, and willow appeared, at first sparsely, then more densely. Soon the creek gushed, full and clear, with snow melt from off distant mountains, and the footing gave way to viscous, sucking mud.

Collins felt the air thin and the pace of the procession slow as they climbed higher. He mused as he rode, daring to dream of women he had known, trying each moment to cloud his longing for Laughing Water with other, more willing faces. The red horse was picking his own way, when suddenly he jerked to a lock-kneed halt. Ahead, the Indian had stopped, too, strung an arrow in his bow, and drawn the bowstring back. At the same time, Drouillard raised his rifle and fired.

The shot cracked like a near burst of lightning. Horses shied and scattered. The red horse humped his back, sprang from all fours high into the air, and surged forward. Rawhide reins raced through Collins's fingers, snapping like loose whips in the air. Collins landed with a grunt in the mud.

The terrified horse raced away, slowed once to jump a loop of the creek, cleared it gracefully, and galloped off over the plateau. Pack horses tried to follow, rushed forward, and tangled their lines in a jungle of willow. The herd scattered. Shouts echoed from the sergeants and captains, and men whipped their mounts to give chase. It didn't last long. Joe Fields's horse reared at the creek. Fields hung on, barely. John Colter's black slowed at the embankment, collected his legs under him, and sprang high as a leggy goat over the water. Colter rose with the thrust to the peak of the arc, but, when the animal arched gracefully back downward, Colter's momentum propelled him straight ahead. He flew smoothly as a bird on the wing, and landed feet first, with a sucking sound, on the opposite bank.

Warner tried to ford the stream. His horse crashed to its knees, and Warner fell. Only Shannon forded the creek successfully, galloped steadily, and gained on the stallion. But his mount swerved suddenly and only a quick handful of mane, kept young Shannon and the horse together as they raced back to the security of the herd.

The stud stopped once on a low rise on the opposite side of the creek. Tail and mane streaming in the wind, head raised defiantly, he posed like the lord he was. Collins wiped his eyes and gawked. Only one sight in his whole life had inspired him with greater awe than a powerful, streamlined horse, and that was Laughing Water. He laughed. The laughter was contagious. Soon general merriment broke out and Sergeant Gass blasted: "If I'd whiskey, gentlemen, I'd say you were drunk!" He guffawed with gusto until the tears dripped from his cheeks into his matted beard. Even Meriwether Lewis bit back a smile. But the Indian sat calmly and took careful note of where the loose horses had disappeared. Finally William Clark bellowed above the din: "To work men, round them up!"

148

Collins pulled himself angrily out of the mud, wiped his face on his sleeve, and with a finger cleared the mud from his ears. He heard Gass screaming at him: "Private Collins, unhorse Private Bratton! That mare's in season an' yon stallion'll be back sniffin' an' fornicatin' sure as me skin is white!"

York was already struggling to loosen Bratton's bindings when Collins pulled him from the mare and a loud whinny trumpeted from across the creek.

Gass bellowed: "Here he comes, the rogue, at the ready!" Tail poised like a waving guidon, the stallion splashed through the water to face Collins who stood firmly in his path.

Collins never heard the sergeant shout: "Outta his way, lad! Man's muscle can be no match!" The horse charged. Collins locked his knees, hips, spine, and braced a shoulder made broad by years of rowing, and dug in his heels. He reached for a rein as the horse galloped by, grabbed it, and jerked. The horse never slowed but dragged Collins on his belly into the creek. When Collins let go, he lunged for the mare.

She squealed and threatened a kick. Resistance only emboldened the stallion that reared and mounted. The coupling was beastly and violent.

Drouillard waited until the act was over, dashed in, and again caught the rein. He yanked hard enough to turn the animal's head when the rein snapped and a yellow glint of liquid anger flared in the stallion's eye. Ears flat, teeth bared, the horse dove for Drouillard. The scout swept up a handful of dirt and threw it at the horse's eyes. It struck the lathered neck without effect, and Drouillard leaped headlong into the creek. The stallion stopped, snorted, sniffed the water, then wheeled and pranced away.

Laughter died quickly when men took count of the chaos one rifle shot had caused. Three men, Collins, Colter, and Billy Warner, had lost their mounts. The pack horses and Bratton's gentle mare had tangled their lines hopelessly in the willow scrub. Billy Warner had bruised the shoulder that had broken his fall. Collins, Colter, and Drouillard were soaked to the bone. But they had been lucky. Injury to pride and reputation as skilled horsemen was easier to mend. They sat in water up to their chests and laughed.

"Rather swim than ride, eh, lads? I give you your paddles back or an apron, you can pluck fowl an' cook." Gass handed Collins a bucket. "And another for you, proud John Colter. There's a good horse will humble every braggin' man. Bring water. Strike the fire. Dry yourselves out while the lads sort the animals an' retrieve the packs." The Irish sergeant expressed no sympathy. To him, pain, if not fatal, was like poverty, to be endured, and teasing, even brutal mockery and criticism was like friendship, always to be accepted with equanimity and sometimes laughter.

Gass bent to pick up Collins's rifle from the creek. The stock had splintered and the barrel bent. Gass pitched the gun to Collins who caught it on the fly. Then the sergeant grumbled: "Can't discard a gun. Shields can wipe it out, brace the stock, put it to right. You've a fair pot of Irish luck, Collins. Could've broken your skull. So much for your expert horsemanship."

Colter gulped a few breaths before he dragged himself to his feet and sputtered: "Another score to settle with our Irish lord an' master."

Collins lay back in the mud, filled his fists with the slop, raised an arm, and hurled it hard at Gass. He missed, and Colter mocked his faulty aim. But Collins tried a second throw and it struck John Colter in the open mouth. Colter spit grit into his hands, clapped them together, slapped them against his thighs, and charged like an enraged bull. The two slipped and slapped in a schoolboy's tussle until Drouillard grabbed Collins by his filthy hair and Labiche grabbed Colter's belt and shoved them both in the direction of the fire.

Drouillard dragged John Collins back to the creek and dunked him again before releasing him. "Now you're washed, we find your horse."

"Let the Indians have him, eat him alive if they please."

Drouillard laughed and replied: "Venison tastes better. You're cold and angry, but you'll dry. The shot that set your horse bucking . . . I shot us a meal. And the Indian's arrow struck more meat for the pot. Tonight we eat and we feast."

Colter slaughtered the two fat bucks, Collins carried water, and the two friends reverted to their herding duties as if never an insult had come between them.

The next morning, the expedition moved on to the bald pate of a high hill where the burning sun baked down and they could see the Snake River writhe and coil toward a fringe of soft hills and distant mountains. The red horse stood peacefully grazing in its loop.

Drouillard set out after him. He was gone all day and only caught up with the column at dusk when Gass stopped him a quarter mile out. "Cap'n wants that horse's hide. Swore he'd shoot him if he lays eyes on 'im. Dirty shame, handsome rogue."

Resisting, Drouillard glared. His deep voice fell to an angry rasp. "He only did what he's bred for."

Gass's blue eyes twinkled. He stroked his beard thoughtfully, leaned close to Drouillard's ear, and tried to contain his Irish screech: "Cap'n can't strike you, Drouillard, if you disobey. You're not in the army. The animal has value. Keep the horse . . . rob him of his jewels . . . do as you will, but don't say I told you."

Drouillard smiled lightly. "Sergeant, you're a scheming wretch. But I'll need Collins."

Collins came, picked up a stone, and began silently to hone his knife, while Drouillard hobbled the stallion on good grass and declared: "You hold him. I'll make the cut." And he mused: "Like robbing him of his soul, enslaving him worse than York." He admired the deep chest, sloping shoulder, and powerfully muscled rump, shook his head, and whispered: "Shame."

Collins met Drouillard's sad glare with a devilish leer. "Don't have to cut 'im. We could let 'im go." He waited for Drouillard to refuse, and, when Drouillard didn't speak, he walked to the horse and removed the hobbles.

The stallion didn't run, but moved away gradually, cropping mouthfuls of grass as he went. A pang seized

152

John Collins like the awful pain he suffered when he'd left Laughing Water and he breathed deeply to relieve the pressure in his chest. Something of beauty and power was exiting his life. The horse swung his head, glared at Collins, nickered, then meandered to a low swale. Collins muttered: "God go with you. They can whip me, if they please, for letting you go."

Drouillard touched his arm. It was time to go back to camp. Collins turned once to look back. The horse was gone. His vision blurred, he closed his eyes and beheld another parting on the mighty Missouri when the graceful Mandans crowded the riverbank. The one face that he wanted most to remember wasn't there. He cursed the day he'd left her and mumbled: "I always lose what I love the most. Why?" His shoulders rounded and his whole stature shrank.

Drouillard observed his pain, lay a hand on his arm, and sympathized. "You'll return to her, *mon ami*, as fast as God and the good river permit."

The corps welcomed them when they returned. Collins let exhaustion envelop him. He ate a spare meal, washed in the river, curled up on ground warmed by the fire, and fell asleep. Drouillard threw a warm hide over him.

Fingers of cold light groped at the horizon when he awakened and a dark image defined itself against an emerging red dawn. It was morning, the wind was up, and York stood over him. The slave had delayed his morning ritual to seek out Collins.

With a wide grin, he began eagerly: "Massa Johnny, afore the sun went down, Injun an' me, we seen your

153

hoss run. I spent many a night, sleepin' in the hay wi' the hosses, hunkerin' under the straw to keep warm, feelin' their breath on my spine, smellin' the steam that rose from their piles. I know a runner an' I know a puller from a packer. That red one's a runner. He run away clean as the wind. I seen 'im go." York shook his head. "I pray the wind will sweep me up, make me run like that. I pray the wind will set me loose."

Collins listened and thought how deep passion, long denied, expanded and resounded with force in the breast of the black man. York, like Collins, had a wife that he loved. The possibility of loss haunted this man more than Collins could imagine. For York, the capricious scratch of a master's pen could destroy life itself. Words stuck in the back of Collins's throat. He blinked and asked: "How can the wind set you free?"

"She tole me when I left, that the wind's God's own breath. Wind blows the distance and the wind will carry my words back to her. An' I speak to her ever' morn."

Collins was silent. Would the wind carry his thoughts to Laughing Water? He wondered and sputtered: "It's a long way home, long way for wind to blow." Then he muttered without comprehending why: "Will it carry my words, too? Can I call on the wind?"

York nodded. "I believe it will blow away to her, Massa Johnny, if she wants to hear."

But Collins stammered an uncertain reply: "Your master is closer. Does your master hear?" Then he blundered: "I'm not your master. Don't call me master."

154

CHAPTER
THIRTEEN

On the last day of April, they began the day's march and rode fifteen miles into treeless hills. Collins's heart was barren as the surrounding land. The west wind blew and Collins whispered softly into it. He kept his voice low so they would not mock him for imitating a slave. If others, especially Cruzatte or Colter heard, they would ridicule and scorn him. Whether or not he believed, whether or not she heard, seemed not to matter because the secret effort settled his heart and made the miles pass more quickly.

April ran into a cool May. The corps made an early camp on May 3rd, six miles below a village of the Walla Walla. Again, handfuls of grass produced a tepid fire. But Yellept, the Walla Walla chief, who had intercepted them on the westbound journey, came to welcome them back. The Walla Wallas were inland Indians who lived at the base of tall mountains. They did not flatten their faces like the river tribes, and, like their cousins on the eastern plains, they raised horses and hunted for meat.

Feathered and beaded, Yellept paraded slowly forward leading a handsome white horse. A long train of attendants, carrying armloads of dry, flammable logs, followed. It had been days since the corps had ignited real wood, months since they had seen a robed chief. The corps stood quietly but enviously as, with a sweep of powerful arm, Yellept motioned his followers to bring the wood forward to the fire and dropped the horse's lead at Meriwether Lewis's feet.

The old chief drew back his shoulders and spoke and Drouillard repeated his words for all to hear: "The white horse is a gift for the captain. They do not expect payment. He bids us visit his village." The explanation met with blank disbelief until Yellept took a log and set it on the pitiful grass fire. Flames lapped the dry bark as the hardwood heated and burst into steady flame. Even at a distance, Collins could feel the heat that penetrated hearts and hands. Then Yellept spread out silken otter skins and invited Lewis and Clark and the officers to sit.

Both Lewis and Clark acceded, and the sergeants and Indian dignitaries, who followed, took their positions like honored guests at an affair of state. The enlisted men gathered eagerly at the fire, warmed themselves, and cooked their meal.

Drouillard, who sat in their midst, raised his voice. "Tomorrow, we'll visit Yellept's village where his people have prepared a feast. We gave him our word we would come on the way downriver. He has not forgotten because his prestige depends on our visit." He concluded: "The horse is white, the color of magic and holy power, and a symbol of his deepest respect."

They marched to the village, but two days of visiting turned into four and the delay provoked complaints

156

that increased in volume and frequency. On the fourth night, Drouillard came to the fire with the Indian herder and a freshly killed beaver and announced: "He can wait no longer. Already others have passed us by. The trail to the Nez Percé, his cousins, is short. He must leave tomorrow with the horses."

The statement, so blunt and so brief, left no room for argument and yet objections rang out loudly.

"A hard lesson, trusting an Injun."

"Rather trust a slave."

"Captain won't take an Injun's word."

Stubbornly Sergeant Gass reminded the protestors: "If the captains had trusted Indians on our way west, we would have been blessed with a shorter, happier route."

Drouillard smiled at that. His hawkish eyes watched the men's faces as he added: "I'm half Shawnee and you trust me. Trust this herder. We shall follow him in the morning."

The Nez Percé herder was true to his word. He conducted them to a large village nestled in the timbered bottom of a rushing creek. On the way there, he pointed out water holes where game animals collected and clearings where grass grew thick and horses grazed and fattened. The Nez Percé villagers came out in welcome. These were the same generous people who had rescued the corps from the terrible mountains only months before. But the corps was poor and could offer no gifts in gratitude.

By contrast, the village was rich. Spacious lodges nestled among the trees and fine horses stood at the entries to lodges. The horses that the expedition had brought west grazed on the high plain. William Clark assigned Colter and Collins to tally those they'd left there the previous fall.

When they rode out to find the herd, Colter remarked: "Only Kentuck horses are prettier, Johnny." The wide pasture and peaceful animals reminded Colter of home.

Collins nodded and smiled, but his thoughts were far from Kentucky or this peaceful scene. Laughing Water was surely prettier. He bit his lip, thinking how he wanted her but for now, if he could not have her, maybe the speed and power of the horse could help tame his restless heart.

With a smirk, Colter guessed the reason for his silence. "She's half a continent away, Johnny and the red one's a renegade. Look at these, thousands of them, solid, sturdy animals, gold to an Injun. You bought your wife with horses, remember? You can buy 'er back or find another with more horses."

Annoyed with himself for letting his feelings show, Collins answered acidly: "Gold's a lump in your bed, Colt. Get it out of your head or you'll get greedy as Charbonneau sleepin' on it." Toussaint Charbonneau's secret gold had incited jealousies on the long journey west when Colter had found gold on a hunting trip.

Colter grinned and rambled on: "Horses gonna buy me a princess, maybe buy a woman who'll kiss Labiche's ugly mug. Gold's more faithful than women."

158

"Labiche could've bought his own wife. He don't want a woman." Collins flipped the sullen reply, but he was glad to shift the emphasis to the pirate.

"Yes, he does. It's women don't want him." Colter's voice seemed a distant echo in an alien reality.

Collins was no longer listening. His mind had conjured Laughing Water, her silken tresses and soft-tanned skin, her touch and smell, so distant, yet so real. All at once, he understood Labiche and the everlasting ache of one who desired but never obtained. Labiche was one of the bravest men he knew, brave as Drouillard, and Labiche had replaced desire with reckless abandon. Could he, John Collins, smother his own craving so completely? He would try on the back of a horse.

Colter interrupted: "How many you count? I count fifty-two."

Collins had been preoccupied and hadn't counted the horses, but he repeated anyway: "Fifty-two. Some's missing." He whipped his horse and galloped back to the village. A bewildered John Colter followed.

The corps had collected in front of the chief's lodge. Men milled haphazardly about while the captains conferred with Bighorn, the Nez Percé chief. Labiche had spread a rawhide square on a level patch of ground and sat cross-legged with Shannon, Gibson, and three Indians playing the old shell game by sleight of hand. Spectators, Indian and white, looked on as Labiche manipulated the nutshells. He jabbed a thumb in the direction of the lodge as Collins and Colter dismounted: "Captain's inside, begging meat. And I will win us more. We'll fill our bellies tonight." He rubbed the deep scar that disfigured his face and cackled. "Told the captain to make the savages pay for his eye water an' Rush's pills . . . that and salt are about all we have left to bargain with." He shook his head. "Lewie called me barbaric for denying help to suffering souls. What an innocent, trusting soul is our fair captain! I told him that even barbarians have to eat. Selling your goods for what it's worth is only right. Barbaric was the devil who cut this scar. Anyway, Clark agreed with me. Go on in. They're waiting." He rolled the dice in his palm and went back to his game.

But no sooner had Collins and Colter approached the entry, than Bighorn and the captains emerged from the lodge into the bright light of day. William Clark was smiling, but Meriwether Lewis's clean-shaven face had contracted in a tight frown. He introduced Bighorn and addressed the entire corps: "Bighorn assures me that the high country is still snowbound. He called the passes 'deep baskets brimming with snow.' Until it melts, we must wait."

Wait — another delay. Collins didn't want to wait. No one did. Audible groans issued from men who wanted to put the mountains behind them, the sooner the better. Their loud protests reverberated.

Lewis pretended not to hear, raised a hand, waited for silence, and resumed: "Until spring comes to the high country, Bighorn has assigned to each mess, a lodge. There you will gather to eat and sleep with your sergeants, who will assign your duties. Be friendly, courteous, and patient. Last year, these same people

160

saved us from starvation, nursed us back to health. Repay their generosity now with your good conduct, co-operation, and friendship. May our wait be short and our time spent, pleasant and peaceful for us and for our hosts." The exhortation was mild and better suited to the conventions of a drawing room. But this was an Indian village and these were hardened frontiersmen.

Lewis was still speaking, scrutinizing his men through narrow slits of eyes, but Collins had long since ceased to hear. The captain's voice droned meaninglessly in his ear as restlessness rolled in like a crashing wave. Collins wanted to reach the Mandans as quickly as possible. Colter wanted to explore the mountains. Everyone wanted to strike out on the trail home.

But Lewis bowed to Bighorn, turned on his heel, and walked majestically back into his lodge. He left Captain Clark to execute and explain to the waiting men.

"Except for hunting, maintaining your weapons, and herding," Clark began, "your time will be your own. Use it wisely. Rest. Mend your clothing. Build your strength." He nodded once and muttered: "Dismissed." That was all. Tough, hardy, young men had to fill their own hours. Distractions, mainly women, were available and willing, even for ugly Labiche.

John Collins shuffled off to a round rock and sat, elbows on knees, chin resting in his hands, glaring into space, resisting the visceral urge to seek out a willing woman. York passed with an armload of wood.

Bratton, who was still unable to walk, rested on his pallet nearby, and observed: "She's makin' a slave o' you, Johnny, like these useless legs have made a slave o' me, just like the blackie, there, haulin' his burden."

Collins hated to admit what he'd tried hard to deny. He muttered irritably: "Who's *she?*"

"That Injun gal, your wife. She's in your heart and in your brain. You'll be happier when you shake her outta your head."

Late into the night, revelry rang in the village. In the hours before dawn, rowdy, exhausted men drifted back to their assigned lodges, staggering to their beds. The sergeants and captains held an early meeting.

"Are all the men accounted for?" Clark posed the question.

Sergeants Ordway, Pryor, and Gass didn't answer. They, too, had been absent all night long. Only Collins, Bratton, York, and Charbonneau, because he had a wife and child present, had remained in their lodges.

Ordway was first to admit: "The men have not all come in yet, sir."

Lewis's rigid restraint crumbled. His lips drew taut, but his words were mild compared to the acid in his voice. "Confine all revelers to their quarters. That, sergeants, includes the three of you."

Drouillard protested loudly: "Sir, confinement will only inflame disobedience and discontent. The winter was long. The women of the river were unappetizing thieves. Labiche's games, Cruzatte's fiddle can never replace the companionship of a good woman." He paused, flicked a knowing glance, then resumed. "The men smell a filly like the red stud horse. And he's back,

162

sir. I saw him with the herd. Please, sirs, allow your corps games, contests, companionship, and good cheer." Drouillard could speak candidly to his captains because he was an independent scout and owed no allegiance to officers of the U.S. Army.

Irishman Gass nodded and winked at Clark. "Sir, there's other distractions besides women, like races an' contests of strength. A wee mite o' competition would entertain fertile imaginations." He crinkled his mild blue eyes, waited for the thought to penetrate, then added: "The natives love a contest. They'd enjoy the diversion, too. What said the bard? A good horse, a lovely woman, bread, song, and wine. We only lack the wine, sir."

Drouillard added persuasion: "Challenge them to a race." He paused and, when Lewis did not object, then cautioned: "They have thousands of horses. We have the white and maybe the red, but we should discover first how they conduct their races."

William Clark sanctioned the race, something to excite men's spirits and refill empty coffers, and he sent Drouillard to deliver the challenge to the village.

"Who shall ride, sir?" Labiche posed the question to Captain Clark. "He should be our best horseman or we will be betting we lose." He meant Collins, but Clark insisted: "Draw lots for the ride . . . Collins, Colter, Warner, and Shannon."

They caught the white horse, but could not find the red. Labiche contributed a fine saddle that he'd won from an Indian, and held sticks for the four riders to draw. Collins drew the shortest and won. He had never ridden the white horse.

He and Drouillard went immediately to try the animal. No one knew when he'd last had a rider. Drouillard held him steady while Collins mounted. Collins urged him forward slowly in a tight circle. The horse was nimble and quick, snorting and kicking. A ripple of muscle sent a shiver from shoulder to tail. Collins widened the circle and lengthened the stride, and the animal's energy built like a tightly wound spring.

Gass and Colter watched closely. Finally impatient Gass shouted: "Turn him loose lad! Let 'im run!"

Collins turned toward the open plain and smacked the white flank with the quirt. The horse leaped forward with a surge of muscle that, but for a fistful of mane, would have left John Collins in the dirt. But he held on, wrapped his long legs tightly around the barrel of the horse, and pushed his weight up off the animal's spine. With each lunging stride, man and horse flew over the plain. Wind, light, time, and pain streaked away. It ended too quickly. Collins threw his weight to the rear and reined back as a wall of trees loomed up before him. The white horse barely slowed, swerved left, and finally halted in the shade of a monstrous fir.

Nez Percé herders witnessed the breakneck dash and sent swift runners to the village. Word of the white man on the flying white horse sped to every ear in every lodge. White rider and white horse combined the magic of gods and ancestors, the speed of the wind, and the light of the sun. Challenges came quickly, so many that

164

Sergeant Gass spent the afternoon organizing heats to determine which would contest the white stallion. And all afternoon, they raced across the broad, level pasture while a frenzy of betting consumed white man and red.

Ordway interrupted a colloquy with Bighorn to inform Captain Lewis: "The horse is fast, sir. The betting is faster and furious."

Lewis's face paled. His lips drew back and his eyes steeled. "I authorized a race, not wagering. Wagering provokes argument and dissension." Lewis stepped out of the lodge, trained his spyglass on the gleaming animal, and spat a curse: "Damn them all. Get them and bring them here." He passed the glass to Clark, hissing: "You see what comes, Will, of hiring pirates and rascals. Collins and Colter, and the blackguard Labiche, have corrupted even Sergeant Gass. We've unleashed a storm on these guileless people."

William Clark, who had admitted Collins to the corps at the suggestion of Drouillard and hired boatman Labiche, winced. Meriwether Lewis had always favored the nine men from Kentucky like the Fields brothers — Joe and Reuben — and Sergeant Pryor. But they were really no different from the rest. An Indian husband had even threatened to murder Ordway. But Lewis did not understand why the inequalities he abetted served to undermine his authority. William Clark had recruited men like Collins, Labiche, Billy Warner, and George Gibson. The expedition could not have come this far without them. Labiche never sickened and never admitted weakness or pain. In the worst conditions, he could rally and encourage. Collins was invariably brave and athletic, a dead shot, competent rider, and swimmer. Colter was equally talented and always faced hardship as a challenge. And Gass, for all his lewd remarks and earthy Irish crustiness, was toughest and best loved of the sergeants.

William Clark waited for Lewis's temper to calm, then gently dismissed Lewis's protestations, saying: "Irishmen love their horses. We agreed, Meri, that boredom would be a worse storm. The horse will tire. So will Collins and Colter. So will they all."

But the Indians did not tire. Their enthusiasm for contest was innate and intense. They had hundreds of fresh horses, drove the wagering to a fever pitch, and pressured the corps to make Collins run again. Even Labiche sensed the folly of it. But he and Gass encouraged the betting. They carved their crude records on soft strips of bark with the point of a knife. They bet buckles, shirts and robes, lances, baskets, and pelts, until the wagered goods piled high. They won continually, and the winnings they amassed inflamed their enthusiasm more.

An innocent question from John Colter shook their confidence. "You seen where they'll run tomorrow? Across some rugged country, not like any track I ever seen . . . not like your grassy pasture, either."

No one had thought to look. They had assumed the final races would occur where they'd run the heats. But the Indians had set markers to define a different, longer course. It was not a groomed track. It began at the edge of the wood and extended over an open plain, a

166

distance of about three miles. It rose and fell like the waves of a sea. The footing varied. Deep sand, clay, shale rock, mud, and shallow water all marred the way. High grass and the stems of the cous lily concealed bogs. There were stretches where the grass grew in clumps that could snag a hoof, and glue-like mud that could snap a tendon like a fragile bowstring.

Colter led Collins and Labiche to a hill overlooking the course. "The crowd, most of the tribe," Colter said, "will watch from here. There's traps, Johnny" — he eyed Labiche — "like there's eddies in the river. Horse can't gallop start to finish."

Labiche's eyes narrowed and he exclaimed: "A race of wits as well as of speed, man and beast against the land, like man and boat against the river! A risk, my friend, as good a gamble as ever." He slapped Collins's back with renewed enthusiasm and blurted: "Ride your best, ride like the wind, Johnny. Watch 'em run their heats. Learn their habits before you run."

All afternoon they watched, and Collins beat down his apprehensions, but they always popped back. He counted between ten and twenty horses for every heat. They milled about a starting line, which was no more than a ragged furrow traced in the sand. The starter held high a lance with a white strip of fur attached and it was up to each rider to watch for the lance to fall, the signal for the race to begin. There were no rules. Galloping horses swerved, dodged, nudged, and pushed. Riders used quirts on man and beast. Horses slowed to cross a bog or descend a steep incline. Many, who didn't, fell or pulled up lame. A win was pure, unadulterated luck. A loss did not discourage the Indians. Losers never gave up, but returned with more horses and more hopes as spectators crammed the overlook above the plain and lined the footpath that ran the length of the course. They shouted encouragement and invective and outshouted each other.

Labiche spent the afternoon with John Colter and Sergeant Patrick Gass, his keen intelligence seeking advantage wherever it tempted. The three men accumulated baskets of the roots, a bridle richly beaded, and a sturdy travois, and they gloated over the winnings. Labiche asserted: "Poor no longer. One horse cannot carry it all home. And tomorrow, Johnny, we bet on you." Collins did not reply.

Gass's head snapped around. He said: "You doubt, Johnny? Risk, my fine lad, is what we all live by. Today, luck has been kind and tonight we feast. Horses have bought us rainbows and good fortune."

Labiche added: "Like I bought you a bride." He kissed the tips of his fingers and tossed the kiss into the wind. "Like maybe I find me a healthy mate among these fine people. They are much like me. They love a game. An' like you, too, John Colter."

Colter replied: "I wager my future on gold, not a horse."

They looked to Collins, but he had turned his face away. His eye fell upon an animal picketed only a few yards behind the low sweeping branches of a giant fir. The horse had a head like a battering ram and legs like pilings. The Indian owner was carefully grooming the

168

mare as she laid her ears back, bared her teeth, and snapped irritably at the man. Collins stared, then laughed, and the laughter turned to pity.

Labiche corrected him. "Not so funny. That mare's their fastest and longest runner. She belongs to Bighorn, the chief."

Collins spat and muttered a curse, but Gass's eyes grew wider as he declared: "Then God and the saints smile upon us."

John Colter overheard and, drawing Collins aside, said: "Bighorn's he says? If she's fast as they say, let her set the pace, find the footing. You save your strength for the last, then challenge her for the final dash. We'll bet her to place, and tonight, Johnny, if we can catch the red stud who has wandered all over this country, we'll make sure we win."

Grinning, Collins agreed: "You think the red one is faster."

Colter winked and added: "Faster and smarter and tougher. I know so."

They walked back to camp, but Sergeant Pryor intercepted them halfway.

"Drove Cap'n Lewis to a fury runnin' his new white horse. Clark told me to tuck the four o' you far away from Lewie's wrath tonight, lest he hauls you all up on charges."

"Charges of what? We were assigned to run the horses."

"The way Lewis sees it, you ran his white horse too hard. Come with me." He led them to a modest lodge where they ate an insipid, boiled meal and bedded for the night.

Gass complained loudly: "A shameful reward for a day's success."

The next day, race day, dawned bright and cool. Before the sun broke the horizon and shed light enough to see, John Colter and John Collins caught the red horse. He was easy to find with his harem of mares. They drove in the mares, and the stallion followed.

Colter remarked: "Don't give a tinker what Lewie thinks." Then he added: "Find the slave. Ask 'im to conjure a lucky wind."

The Indians had driven in herds of shaggy mountain beasts and begun to sort and saddle their mounts before the corps headed out to the racecourse. As Collins watched, his anxiety grew. To assess a horse's ability when his muscle and bone were hidden beneath a hairy winter's coat and camouflaged by these Indian horses' peculiar speckling was difficult. As for the Indian riders, they were able and daring to a man.

When the sun was at its zenith, the starter shrieked his summons. John Collins mounted and edged the red stallion into the mêlée at the start. Horses crowded and bumped, and Collins struggled to keep the red horse from charging the line. He saw Bighorn's ugly mare at the far right of the pack, ears laid back, teeth bared, threatening, vicious. Horses and riders recognized her belligerence and let her alone.

The lance fell. The mare was first off the mark. Collins's red horse plunged forward an instant later.

170

From the right, a brown horse charged across Collins's path. Collins reined back, jerked left. The stallion slowed, but barely veered. He had spied the mare, locked on her scent, and thundered after; Collins could not hold him.

The mare splashed through a bog. Mud flew from her hoofs into the stallion's eyes. Like the slap of a glove, dirt in his face only incensed the red horse. But the mud splattered Collins's eyes, too, so that he could barely see the mare as she exited the bog and weaved between scattered rocks. Her stride was even, relentless, and swift, and her gait was smooth. Horses mired or fell behind, but, like a streak of fire, the red stallion charged on and gained on the mare.

Collins took a hand from the rein to wipe his eyes and dared look back. A mud-spattered charger, black as night, ran steadily behind him. No other horse was in sight. Doubt turned to hope, then confidence, then wild elation gripped Collins's heart.

The mare slowed and surged right. Collins seized the moment to lay his quirt to the flank and pass her by. When he struck, the stallion surged, but Collins barely saw the ditch before he felt the hocks reach beneath him and the supple spine contract to jump. The horse was in the air at the peak of a giant leap above the gaping pit; Collins was balanced evenly over the powerful shoulders. The stallion plunged down, his forelegs straightened to land, but the force of his landing drove his hoofs deeply in heavy mud. Like hammered stakes, they stuck fast. Collins pulled his knees to his chin and threw himself free as the horse's

171

rear flipped over his proud head in a flying somersault. Behind him, the big black also gathered the force to jump. He checked himself before taking off, but also bogged on landing and crashed into the red stallion. His rider flew high over Collins's head. Shaking and snorting, both horses rolled and rose and rushed away to escape the pack that was galloping down. But the riders could not escape quickly enough. The Indian wound himself into a tight ball and Collins did the same as flying hoofs flicked past. More horses that could not swerve slipped and piled in the deep mud. Riders and spectators shook their fists at Collins who they blamed for the pile-up.

Collins scrambled to the sidelines and shrank from the uproar. Colter caught the red horse. Together, they retreated to a lonely spot along the creek to avoid the sight of the disaster and the remonstrances of their fellows.

Labiche, jovial as always, sought them out. "What did I tell you, Johnny . . . she is their fastest horse, an ugly, clever one like me."

Collins stared at the sky and at the ripples in the river. Slowly the truth seeped into his perceptive brain. Labiche had hedged and had bet on the mare. Collins blistered with anger. Colter, too, understood, balled his fists, and sprang at the pirate who dodged and ran away, laughing.

Sergeant Gass came to them then. "You did as much as any man, Johnny lad. The Lord be thanked that you an' Colter are whole. Humiliation is worse torment than defeat." He added: "Pirate's gone to celebrate with the natives. Come with me. The men still love the two of you. 'Tis Cap'n Lewie cannot abide either one o' you."

The corps welcomed Collins and Colter into the circle by the warmth of the central fire. Bratton muttered a solace from his pallet, and Clark came to check Collins for injuries.

Later, Drouillard, mentor and friend, sought the two men out. "Hunt with me, *mes amis*. Change the scenery and keep away from Lewis's wrath."

Both Collins and Colter accepted with pleasure.

CHAPTER
FOURTEEN

The hunters stayed out for four days until William Clark convinced Meriwether Lewis that no article of war had been breached and healthy young men needed diversion. Besides, the Indians had honed the joy of winning and dignity of losing to a high art. Friendships formed in the wake of Collins's loss. More races on foot and horse, more contests of strength and speed occurred in the coming days. Chief Bighorn applauded the games and described to the captains the route they would soon be traveling. It led directly through the highest peaks to the Great Falls of the Missouri and was mercifully short.

On May 16th, when men of Sergeant Pryor's mess gathered around the fire, the night was cold and the fire burned with an eerie glare. Collins sat with Whitehouse, Colter, and Shannon. Bratton lay on his pallet by Cruzatte who drew his bow gently across the worn strings of his fiddle. Long shadows danced across the downcast creases of men's faces. Collins squinted absently, repeating the sounds of letters that Whitehouse drew patiently with a stick in the sand. Colter sewed a torn moccasin. Suddenly the fire flared and sent a tongue of fire leaping into the blackness.

Fresh from Lewis's briefing, Pryor stepped against the backdrop of flames. "Four days to the falls, boys." He shook his head in disbelief. "Same crossing took us eight weeks on the way out." He repeated: "Four days, and then sixteen miles to White Bear Island where we cached the tobacco. We'll be smoking tobacco in June an' lifting a jug in July in Saint Louie."

Men stared in disbelief. Memories were raw of starvation and freezing cold, of cactus thorns that punctured the hard calluses of weary feet, hailstones that bruised and pounded sore muscles and bones, and White Bear Island that spanned the base of not one waterfall, but five.

When the news evoked no reply, Pryor teased: "Want to make your beds here in an Indian lodge?"

Collins flicked a derisive glance and muttered: "Not here, but I'll make my bed in a Mandan lodge." He wanted nothing more than to reunite with his Mandan wife. John Colter in his boundless curiosity and lust for gold would've stayed, too, and, here, York enjoyed the simple freedoms that every Indian accorded him that he could never expect in the white settlements. Labiche, too, feared the impressment crews and had vowed never again to live in a port city, even a river port. Others feared the dangers of the journey, while still others let ignorance reinforce their confidence and had not permitted themselves to think at all. They gathered around the fire, sang their songs, clapped their rhythms, and stomped their dances.

But Collins grew more disheartened daily. Drouillard tried to cheer him. "It's you who impose privation on yourself. Take a woman. Bighorn wants us to mate and be fruitful and enjoy the budding of the land while we are here. Laughing Water and her customs do not forbid it. It's you who punish yourself."

John Collins had a blunt answer. "I forbade her coupling with another. She deserves the same loyalty from me." But abstinence only added to the power of her image and increased his burden of blame now, when he asked himself not if he would see her again, but when.

Drouillard did not try to change his mind. He said: "You've thought long and hard. I hope you see her sooner not later. I will alert you as soon as we are ready to leave. Bighorn will tell us when."

But Bighorn would raise his long arm, sweep it in a wide arc, and shake his wise old head. "My scouts tell me, not until the snows melt and the way is clear." His long braids were white, his brow wrinkled with benevolent concern, and the gravity of age imbued his words. He sat with the captains daily, passed the pipe, bowed his proud head, and promised a guide when the time to leave was at hand. And he asked a favor in return. "The Blackfeet savages who pillage our villages, you must tame them for us. Meet with them, talk to them, and counsel them. Teach them to share the buffalo of the eastern pastures with their western brethren." He ignored the deep worry lines in Meriwether Lewis's brow and continued boldly: "The Blackfeet, who shoot the guns that British traders bring, will listen to you who also have fire sticks."

Lewis could not offend his gracious host, although he wanted sorely to refuse. He'd heard the stories from Shoshones and Flatheads and these generous Nez Percés, and witnessed the glint of terror in their eyes. At the very word, Blackfeet, they turned their heads away and cast down their eyes lest the white man detect the unmanly dread in their faces. The apprehension had spread quickly to the corps, especially to the men from Kentucky whose fathers and brothers had died fighting Shawnees or Cherokees. Some had themselves witnessed the destruction and murder.

In vain, Meriwether Lewis looked to Clark for a reason to avoid the mission. Clark sat cross-legged, staring at a hole in the heel of his moccasin. Bighorn waited for an answer. The soil was warming, the sun moving implacably north on the horizon, and Lewis needed guides to assure quick, safe passage over the peaks.

Finally the old chief drew his own conclusion. "I will wait at the hot springs for news of your success and bring word back to my people."

Reluctantly Meriwether Lewis nodded once and murmured: "I will ask the Blackfeet for peace and send you word." But he could only send word if he were still alive. His face blanched and his voice fell to a nervous whisper as he added: "If I do not come, you will know it is because I cannot. You have my word. We must leave in three days. Have your guides ready."

Bighorn frowned and swept his hand palm down across the space before him, but Lewis had closed his weary eyes.

Drouillard spied the motion and relayed its significance around the camp. "The chief warns of steep trails and deep snows, and Lewis does not heed." He tossed a stick at the fire that promptly roasted to cinders, then added: "There are those among us who would crumble to thin ash." He meant Bratton. The smithy's spirit had lifted and he had regained some movement, but his legs would still not support even his reduced weight and no remedy known to the captains could cure the paralysis.

One cool evening, Drouillard stood over Bratton and offered an unpalatable alternative. He said: "You can stay here with these good people."

Bratton responded with gusto. "You can leave Johnny . . . leave Colter . . . leave the slave . . . but not me. If I die, amen, so be it, but I'm coming with you."

Drouillard heard and announced: "Bratton has reclaimed his will to live."

A deadly silence ensued until young George Shannon prompted: "We could sweat out Bratt's poisons. The Indians do it."

John Shields, the other smithy and friend of Bratton's, disapproved. So did Clark himself, but he left the decision to Lewis, who considered a moment before deciding. "Quackery, perhaps, but a sweat cured the paralyzed Enesher man and gained us our first horse. If only to distract and pass the time, it will provide honest diversion for the men." He rubbed his tired eyes and asked: "Does Bratton subscribe to the experiment?"

"That he does, sir, heartily."

All hands hove to the effort. They dug a deep pit, bent green saplings to form a dome above, and heated rocks to line the gaping hole. Whitehouse wove a strong harness. York rubbed Bratton's skin smooth with fish oil and strapped in his shrunken limbs. Collins and Labiche carried water that they poured over the steaming rocks, then lowered Bratton in and covered the dome with skins to contain the steam. When Bratton choked on the heat or gagged from the smell, they drew him out and submerged him in the icy water of the creek. He rattled from cold and panted from heat. They repeated the curious procedure as long as Bratton's strength and breath permitted. Gradually involuntary spasms started to excite his muscles. After four submergings, he could stand, and, after six, he walked a few shuffling steps.

Collins and the corps looked on in silent amazement until Joe Whitehouse exclaimed: "Lazarus rising from the dead!" He slapped Collins hard in the small of his back.

But Drouillard cautioned: "He's still too weak for a mountain crossing."

During the next days, York shadowed Bratton's every move lest he weaken and fall. Three days later, Bratton stood in the muster line in the place beside Collins that had been empty too long. And when Lewis ordered the assault on the mountains to begin, he took special note of Bratton. "You needn't walk. We go by horse. Welcome back, Private Bratton."

The whole month of May and part of June, they waited to recommence the journey. June 10th, in the afternoon, they set out with enthusiasm and vigor, but without Bighorn's approval or his promised guides, and they soon bogged in snow neck-deep. Men and horses sank and trembled with cold and wet, and Labiche threw Pryor's prediction back in his face. "A smoke of tobacco in June? A glass of whiskey in Saint Louie in July? We're gaggin' on ice an' inhalin' the splinters."

With heavy hearts, they turned back to the village. New doubts that the huge quantities of snow would ever melt compounded impatience and frustration. To dull their worry, men flung themselves into greater revelry than before. Collins ran, swam, rode, and gamed. He clapped and stomped when Cruzatte fiddled. And he took a woman and arched his body to her lithe form, but his thoughts ranged always to his Laughing Water. He ran his fingers through this woman's hair mindful only of the silken tresses of his far-off wife. He imagined her staring, scolding up at him through the eyes of the Nez Percé woman in his bed. He called the woman Laughing Water in the Mandan language that she could not decipher and that he wanted desperately to repeat lovingly, later, to living, breathing Laughing Water. He stroked her smooth skin and fondled soft breasts, as if to rehearse the ecstasy of reunion with the one woman he loved. And all the while he held the secret of his aching desire deeply in his heart.

Labiche remarked to Drouillard: "Johnny's heart is cured as we've cured Bratton's legs."

180

Drouillard denied it. "He smothers his pain and he suffers more for it."

On June 24th, Indian scouts returned with excellent news. The passes were clear. The promised guides were ready. On June 25th, an hour after sunrise, they began the climb. When they reached the pass where a month earlier they'd turned back, the noon sun blared down on the shiny wet surface of snow that had only melted completely at the base of the trees where tiny, yellow glacier lilies bloomed. Their delicate heads gleamed like tempting nuggets of gold. The trail itself was still covered with snow that had thawed and crusted enough to support the weight of a horse. They pressed on up steep inclines and along the rims of frightful crevasses. Horses stumbled and men fell, but the Indian never erred.

Five days later, on June 29th, they descended a steep mountain trail to the hot springs and safety. Hoots of joy greeted the sight of the steam rising from the springs. Men rushed to hobble their horses, unload their packs, jump in, and warm the icy blood in their veins. The captains joined them. Joe Fields shot a fat deer that came to lick salt. Labiche, Charbonneau, and his little wife collected wood, and Bratton lit a hot fire. Colter and Collins butchered and spitted the meat, and they all ate till their stomachs would hold no more, then fell soundly asleep.

Only the captains huddled together far into the night. Meriwether Lewis had not forgotten the purpose which Thomas Jefferson had assigned him: to find a

Northwest Passage to divert valuable Canadian furs away from the British forts and into American hands. And he remembered his promise to Bighorn.

When the corps was fast asleep, he fanned the fire alive and sat glaring at the flames until his eyes pained. His spine curved forward, his head drooped like a heavy ball, and his watery blue eyes blinked at the brightness when he called William Clark to his side. "Time to seek out the Blackfeet, Will. I must speak for Bighorn. I must test the Missouri's northern tributaries." He poked a red-hot coal with the point of his knife and watched it sputter and die. He could not read Clark's expression hidden as it was by deep shadows and a hairy growth of beard. "Will, we must separate. We must split the expedition. I gave Bighorn my word. I will deliver our message of peace to the Blackfoot nation, then follow the Marias River to the fiftieth parallel north. You must go south and take a safer course."

Clark's bass voice issued haltingly from out of the darkness. "Meri, you don't have to go."

The suggestion appalled Lewis. He whispered: "But I gave my word."

Still Clark protested: "Then we must all go with you. The Blackfeet are murderers. Only a large party will impress them and insure your safety."

Lewis stared at the flames until his eyes began to water and the liquid began to drip down a cheek. Then he turned toward Clark and said: "Murderers is what the British have made them, plying them with whiskey and guns, like the Iroquois and the Shawnees. This is why I must go to speak of peace. And you must not go, so that one of us is sure to return and the news of our exploits will not vanish like ash in the wind. If I don't go, the land, the animals and their furs, the rivers, the forests, and plains and wonders we have witnessed will be British, pillaged by British overlords for their endless wars and profits. The Shoshones, the Flatheads, the Nez Percés, the Mandans, all will suffer. We owe them better."

Clark sat still as stone.

Lewis's voice deepened with strong conviction. "There is no passage to the northwest seas, but, if I can persuade the Blackfeet to bring their furs south to American traders who will pay them a higher price, if I can persuade them to live in peace, we will not have come this way in vain." His voice rose prophetically as if a confluence of fates had ordained his mission: "I must go, Will. I ask for your blessing."

Clark formed his answer slowly. "Go then, if it is a duty that, left undone, would cause you regret." He could not meet Lewis's steely gaze.

Lewis wrung sweating hands together to stop their trembling and persisted: "And your blessing?" When Clark did not reply, Lewis nodded sadly and mumbled: "I will seek volunteers in the morning." Slowly he rose and went to his bed.

William Clark lingered. A coal cracked and black smoke from the fire blew into his face. He rubbed his stinging eyes and waited for a breeze to clear the smoke. He whispered aloud to himself: "You, William Clark, you must lead these men home, and see that his death will not be in vain." The weight of responsibility hung heavily on his shoulders. He was only a lieutenant. The Department of War of the young republic had never conferred the rank of captain on William Clark, although Meriwether Lewis persisted in calling him captain and presented him as such to the corps. But if Lewis died, would the War Department believe the word of a mere lieutenant and underling whose enlisted men all called him captain. Or would they accuse him of presumptuous ambition?

In the morning, the sergeants called a muster and men lined up eagerly. Their clothing of skins hung raggedly, but their weapons were polished and cleaned, their chins high, and their backs straight. When Lewis explained his mission and requested volunteers, Collins and Labiche stepped forward as did many others. Lewis chose six: Drouillard, the two Fieldses, Warner, Frazer, and Sergeant Gass.

Later at breakfast, Labiche admitted: "He wouldn't have chosen you, Johnny, but you would have gone. So would we all."

Two more days they waited to rest the horses. On July 3rd, at dawn, Drouillard came to sit beside Collins. He began: "So we part, Johnny." He laid a fatherly hand on Collins's shoulder, pressed, and said: "Serve your captain well as I would serve him. That will not be difficult with Captain Clark." The sounds of York's morning prayer echoed faintly in the high mountain air and Drouillard added: "Tell him to beg the wind for our safe return."

184

Collins nodded and threw his arm around Drouillard's stiff neck and hugged him tightly, saying: "And you listen to the wind for me calling you."

Drouillard gave him a quizzical look and whispered: "If I don't come back, *mon ami*, I'll remember you in heaven or hell." Minutes later, he rode away with Lewis and the other five.

Collins heaved a bucket of water at the fire, kicked dirt over the dying embers, and went for his horse. As he mounted, he mumbled: "Six men and a doubtful captain against the war parties of the Blackfeet."

Labiche overheard and answered with a crooked grin: "Lucky seven wins." He shook his head. "Seven. With the captain, they are seven, Johnny."

CHAPTER
FIFTEEN

Ian Parrish, the *Phoenix*'s carpenter, picked up a knot of wood and carved a face while he weighed his options carefully. He liked the feel of the wood, hard and smooth, in his hands. He liked the smell of fir and the feel of solid earth beneath his feet. He'd had enough of the sea. The constant sway and imbalance of a ship in water, the monotonous food, stale water, abbreviated hours of sleep, and punishing work unnerved him. Life indentured to a ship's captain was too like slavery. Since joining Ochoa, he had two small caches of furs that he'd hidden at intervals along the river, even though now these had likely been overrun with natives or washed away with the spring flood. But a larger cache he'd located in a dry cave in a cliff side behind a waterfall, hidden from prying eyes, ample distance above the river. The great carved face that the natives called She Who Watches guarded the spot. The natives feared the power of the ancient carving and visited it rarely, if at all.

Thoughts of Markham, the pompous British captain, and of the good ship *Phoenix* brought a cynical smile to his lips. Ships had returned to the estuary, one Spanish and two British, but none captained by Captain

Markham. To return to one of these would mean the punishment of the deserter — death.

His smile broadened when he thought of Ochoa. The wily half-breed had never anticipated going back. He was content here among these strange people, too content to suspect the secret machinations and true fealty of his subordinate. And so Ian Parrish hatched his treacherous plan.

A Scotsman by birth, white by sire and dam, Parrish detested the freakish natives. He detested Ochoa for his dark skin and the shadowy cast of his brown eyes. Markham's eyes were worse still, icy cold and pale blue. Parrish spat and willed Markham to the hottest fires of hell. A pompous Orangemen, a man very like Markham, had cast Parrish's grandfather, first-born of the Laird of Donismere, from the ancestral home in Scotland. The old man had died in poverty, vowing revenge. Parrish's father had lived his whole life scheming to restore his title and the House of Stuart to the throne of Scotland. Young Parrish spent endless nights by the turf fires in the warmth of his father's gaze, listening to endless stories of the Pretender and Mary, Queen of Scots. Ian Parrish came to love the swing of the kilt, the bleat of the pipes, and the smell of heather on the moors, and to suspect the intentions of the heartless British overlords. These old memories traveled with the young Scotsman. But as for returning to Scotland, he'd been away so long that the few personal connections he'd had had long since evaporated.

Parrish had been eighteen, one year short of fulfilling his seven-year indenture, when the impressment crew had seized him. A frigate, the HMS *Rose*, had lost a mainmast and a dozen able men who washed overboard during a coastal storm. The ship had limped into port for refitting, and the captain, eager to set sail again without jeopardizing his command, sent out the usual gangs to replenish his depleted crew. He would have preferred experienced seamen from merchant ships in the port, but these men had fled the pubs nearest the docks at the slightest whiff of the gang. Unsuspecting young men, like Parrish, had become the hunted prey.

He remembered exactly the day and the hour they had taken him — Monday, July 6, 1796, in the early afternoon. He had been delivering a chair to Dame Cameron, who ran a profitable boarding house that fronted on the harbor. Her clients were mostly sailors on leave, and a few henpecked husbands of the town. She had not been a wealthy lady, but lived comfortably and had seemed friendly enough. After he had set the chair next to the hearth, she had invited him to take tea. She had raised a leaf in the gate-leg table and clapped for her serving girl, a sprightly young thing with bobbing curls, who had smiled at Parrish. He had sat facing a tall clock. He knew the value of hardwoods and had admired loudly its beautiful mahogany case and silky-smooth veneer. Silently he had approved the bouncy servant girl. And he had delighted in the pungent aroma of the tea. Dame Cameron had winked as she poured from her china pot, then reached for a crystal decanter — "Stronger spirits," she had explained, "for such a handsome, virile, young man." She had added a few drams to his tea. Parrish had warmed to the flattery and gulped his tea. It had had a potent, sugary taste. The clock had chimed two. The *clang* had hammered between his temples like the echo of a distant drum, and the gentle *tick-tock* had bleated like bagpipes on the moors. That was all he remembered.

He had awakened in darkness. The air smelled of the rich decay of sodden wood, rotting fish, and low tide. He had been conscious of a sloshing sound and had had the strange sensation that his whole world was rocking. A door had opened above his head and blinding sunlight crashed in. He had blinked and covered his eyes as a raucous voice called: "Bloke's awake! Shall I bring 'im up, sir?" The man had shoved a ladder down and squawked: "Hand yerself outta there, laddie, an' we see what ye be good for."

Blinking, teary-eyed, Parrish had scrambled up into fresh air. He had emerged into a world of rigging and spars, halyards, bells, hardtack, and endless sea, which would define his life for the next ten years.

The first mate had learned of his skill with wood and set him briskly to work under the supervision of the ship's carpenter, who turned out to be a kinder overseer than his dryland master. Eventually Captain Loring of the HMS *Rose* had recommended him to his friend, Captain Markham of the *Phoenix*, whose carpenter had died of fever. Markham was a capricious, sometimes foolish, but not cruel captain.

But Parrish had never forgiven the British Navy for abducting him. And he reveled in the tales of Scottish adventurers like explorer, Alexander MacKenzie, who'd traced the Frazer River to its source and traversed this northern continent from Atlantic to Pacific. He knew that, across North America, Scotsmen were enriching themselves in the fur trade, reserving a percentage of profits for themselves as just recompense for the forfeiture of their homeland, at the expense of the overbearing North West and Hudson's Bay companies. Parrish made up his mind to join them.

He'd heard that Scottish traders resided with the powerful Blackfoot nation and controlled a profitable trade, but that they resided east of the mountains. It would be a fearful trek trying to reach them over the distant mountains. Parrish swallowed hard whenever he contemplated the effort. But he had made the acquaintance of several Chinooks who came regularly to trade on the river and could guide him along the way. If the Chinooks were able, surely he, a hale and healthy Scotsman, could weather the journey to the Blackfoot nation.

It was now late spring. The snows were melting in the high country. Parrish interrupted his thoughts momentarily to stare at his carving. It was an anthropomorphic image that resembled the face on the rocky outcrop. Had he become so accustomed to the deformities of these savages that he envisioned only the pie-faced, wide-eyed glare of a denizen of the river? The thought depressed and repelled him. He frowned

190

at his handiwork and cast it aside. Time to rid himself of Ochoa and escape this savage land.

First, he sought a capable guide among the tribes who flocked to the river from the vast Columbia drainage and brought horses, hides, and furs, which they exchanged for salmon, baskets, and the metal wares that the ships supplied. Parrish spotted one such itinerant trader among the Chinooks. The man's eyes widened when Parrish displayed a sample pelt from his cache. It was exactly the reaction that Parrish anticipated.

The Indian immediately inquired: "And where are the rest?" He was tall like Ochoa and came from an inland tribe. The Chinooks called him Ugly because his face was not flat but angular, and his large nose hooked at a right angle, sharply as a jabbing elbow. Parrish surmised he must have broken it because it whistled with every breath he inhaled.

Parrish replied: "Take me to the Blackfoot nation and I will tell you where the furs are so you can take possession on your return."

By mid-May, Ugly had completed his trades and started back upriver, and Parrish abandoned Ochoa for good and went with him. They moved swiftly and followed established trails along the river until they reached the same route inland that the expedition had taken. Only once did Ugly propose a detour when he learned that Americans were visiting his people.

Parrish brought out a rich pelt of the sea otter and tempted. "This is yours if you will pass your people by."

191

And so they pressed on, avoiding contact with Americans and consequent loss of time. But Ugly stopped just short of Bighorn's village and encamped with a family in a pleasant, secluded glade, on the banks of the Lapwai River. Here, for a time, like the expedition, they remained to gather horses and supplies and build their strength until the snows cleared from the passes. They did not wait very long.

The perilous climb over the mountains began on June 20th. Parrish was snoring and sleeping soundly when Ugly pulled back his warm fur blanket and summoned: "Come now. The snow has crusted enough to hold our weight."

Parrish cursed and wondered if he had not fled one overlord for another, but he obeyed. They left within the hour and climbed a slippery, switchback trail. The sun was high. At midday, when the snow was softest, they rested, then continued when temperatures dropped and a solid surface froze. Ugly set a grueling pace and took advantage of every glimmer of twilight to continue the march. His stamina was remarkable and his vision never erred. Parrish rode one horse and led another and wrapped himself in pelts to fend off the numbing cold.

The Indian did not slow when they reached the hot springs days ahead of the expedition and clambered down the Missouri to the Sun River. There he turned north. Parrish learned the reason for his haste later from Larkin, the irascible Scots-Irishman who traded for the Hudson's Bay Company with the notorious Blackfeet.

Larkin chewed his pipe stem as he complained: "You told him where you cached your furs. He wants to return this summer to open your caches and sell the rest of your furs to the ships' people. He will be a rich man." Larkin did not offer a smoke to Parrish whose nostrils sniffed enviously. Instead the trader's lip curled ominously as he exhaled, then resumed: "You should have retrieved your treasure, sold the furs yourself, or brought them with you." Still he did not offer tobacco to Parrish whose eyes watered from the smoke.

The accusation was harsh. Parrish did not contest and he let Larkin ramble on.

Larkin puffed and obliged eagerly: "Your Indian guide fears the Americans have already penetrated your cache and traded your furs for food and transport. He says they are a penurious lot, that they have very little that is their own and that it is only through theft and chicanery that they have come so far. 'Tis a miracle that they've survived this long. Can you say where they spent the winter?" Larkin had been informed of the Americans on their outbound journey and was curious to learn all that Parrish knew.

But Parrish withheld his knowledge. It was his only leverage with the suspicious Scotsman and he measured his response carefully. "I saw them heading upriver. The natives tell me that they came from the east, but the river natives are not reliable witnesses, and I doubt their word."

Larkin smiled. "'Tis a pleasure for me to speak English and not have to repeat myself." He returned immediately to the subject at hand. "My scouts tell me the Americans have horses." He paused to lend gravity to his next pronouncement. "Did you know that they were on the Clearwater only a few short days behind you? They've Nez Percé guides and sturdy mounts." He frowned and patted his thick red beard. "There's thirty or more with ample horses, guns, and powder."

Parrish was silent. He could not enhance what Larkin already knew.

Larkin motioned him to follow and ushered him to an adjacent lodge, past two gruff natives with guns, and threw open the lid of a long wooden crate. It was filled to the brim with British muskets. He declared smugly: "My warehouse. I keep it well-guarded. I told my superiors that I needed to arm these people to thwart a Spanish threat, but Americans will make a likelier target."

They returned to the home lodge where Parrish sank into a soft cushioned chair, smiled, and settled comfortably. Larkin removed a second pipe from a sack hanging on a lodge pole and pitched it with a pouch of tobacco into Parrish's lap. He produced a bottle that he promptly uncorked. "A smoke . . . the native custom is almost civilized . . . and for a fellow Scotsman, a dram." Parrish filled his pipe eagerly as Larkin passed the bottle, sat back, and sputtered in a cloud of smoke. "One year ago, maybe more, Rupert Bunch, the company's factor with the Assiniboin, alerted me about the American expedition, and my own scouts spied them slogging upriver in the sweltering Missouri breaks."

194

Parrish lifted the bottle to his lips and set it down with a quizzical look as Larkin elucidated.

"A strange name . . . breaks . . . white sandstone cliffs that confine the river and intensify the summer heat. Perfect oven, the riverbed in August, no worse hell on earth." Parrish wiped his mouth on his sleeve and did not drink more. Larkin scrutinized his sober, taciturn guest, then continued: "My scouts did not confront them. They preferred to let them bake and fry." He waited for a response.

Parrish tamped tobacco into the bowl of his pipe, returned a level gaze, then spoke: "You are telling me they died . . . that these Americans are not the same men?"

Larkin shrugged.

"Then who are they?"

"Men from Spain, Russia, a competing British or Dutch company, freebooters, Boston men who've landed to usurp our trade in furs. Exploration, discovery, the excuses they would have us believe are all lies. Twenty-three years ago, Britain abandoned her colonies. Now the former colonies consort with the French tyrant and Napoleon has a wide reach." Parrish pretended comprehension. Larkin laughed. His face reddened and his voice rose in pitch and volume. He slammed a tightened fist against his thigh. "Bloody little Corsican sold them Louisiana to create a thorn in the side of Britain. But they have been only a tiny scratch to the Hudson's Bay and the British crown. That they remain so, that the thorn does not fester, we must make certain and bury them in their savage soil."

With a flourish, he raised his glass and declared: "God save the King."

Parrish repeated the toast with gusto so as not to offend his host, but he knew little of the affairs of the Hudson's Bay Company and cared less about the British crown. Parrish repeated: "Who are they?"

Larkin answered with a dismissive wave: "These cannot be the same persons who came upriver stumbling and falling like raindrops. They are Shoshones, Bannocks, a weak and humble tribe. If they are white, then they are the ragged remnants of mutineers. I've a fair nose for the mutinous stench." Larkin wrinkled his nose and cast a knife-like glance at Parrish.

Parrish stammered defensively: "They have guns."

The haughty trader grinned and answered: "I will send my best scouts, warriors, to find them, whoever they are, and kill them and bring me their furs." His eyes narrowed menacingly. "You, Mister Parrish, will go with them and guard the furs. See that my good Blackfoot subjects do not pilfer and steal. And bring scalps. Prove to me that they are dead and that you will be a good and faithful servant."

It was a death sentence, although Parrish did not know it. His scalp matched exactly the white scalps of the men of the corps. It served to temper the Indians' defeat, two men killed at the hands of four lonely whites — Meriwether Lewis, George Drouillard, and Reuben and Joseph Fields. The Indians could boast to having killed at least one and to have banished the Americans from the Blackfoot hunting grounds.

CHAPTER
SIXTEEN

In early July, William Clark and twenty-one men headed overland down a broad valley. The bitteroot was in full bloom, the trail easy, and the wind warm. The bleats and cries of animals, all the noises of the valleys replaced the lonely silence of the mountains. It was the mating season. Birds called and buffalo roared. Hunting improved. Each man had a horse to ride, meat in his belly, and a buffalo hide to ward off the damp when he slept. Clark jogged alongside his troopers, first one, then another, encouraged, inquired about health and home. With each passing mile, the possibility of success loomed larger, and men responded with their hopes and ambitions. But now one third of the corps was absent, with Captain Lewis exploring the Marias River and seeking the powerful Blackfeet nation, and they were sorely missed. For Collins, the loss of his mentor, Georges Drouillard, hung heavily on his spirit.

The column wound its way through an evergreen forest along the bank of a narrow river. Sergeants Ordway and Pryor headed the column. Clark followed with Charbonneau and his family. The rest marched in line, singly or by twos, except for Collins, Colter, and young Shannon who herded the extra horses in the rear. Collins rode alone for much of the time. He missed the companionship and co-operation of the boats, but the enforced solitude allowed him to screen his heartache from the eyes of others.

Every day at noon, at night before he slept, or in the early dawn before he mounted to gather the herd, he grew more troubled. Labiche, his fellow crewman, first noticed his silences and complained to Sergeant Pryor. "He spends too much time alone. Talks to horses more than men."

Pryor had more pressing problems. He replied: "He's my best herder."

But soon, Collins failed to come in for meals and his absence aroused concern. Early on a hot afternoon, the men sat beneath the heavy shade of a tall cottonwood at the edge of the stream. Collins had not come in. Labiche stood barefooted in the water and started the chatter.

"Where's Johnny? He makes excuses . . . strays, bears, wolves howlin' an' growlin' after a lame foal. He's lonely."

Nearby, Gibson filled a bucket and drank, grumbling: "Sitting on that fancy red horse, he's dreamin' an' starin' at clouds. Horse wanders an' eats. An easy life compared to salt-makin'." Everyone drank and he poured the remaining water over his head.

Joe Whitehouse, who was bathing in the river, shook off the water and called: "Strays, you say, he lost one this morning! Shannon's lookin' for it now!" Whitehouse faced the river and didn't see Collins come up behind him. He turned and snapped his mouth shut.

The banter stopped, and they stared. Sergeant Pryor finally spoke: "You heard, Collins. Why you makin' a hermit of yourself?"

Collins didn't answer.

Pryor gave a dismissive nod and turned to Whitehouse. "Take his place with the herd, Joe." And to Collins: "You stay here with us."

Collins came alive suddenly. He fired back: "Sir, I've done my job. You've no call to punish me."

"It's called looking out for you, Private, not punishing."

Gibson snapped suddenly: "Whitehouse don't waste his dreams on an Injun squaw. Heard she pitched you out, cursed your seed, set you runnin' over river ice at night. That true?"

Collins's face soured suddenly. He balled a fist and lunged at Gibson, who threw up his hands in defense as Sergeant Pryor jumped between them, caught, and pinned Collins's arms.

"Private, cool off, eat a meal, go for a swim." He handed Collins a full plate.

The red flush of anger rose over Collins's handsome face, and Labiche warned: "Blowin' on a hot fire, spreadin' flame where there was none, Gibson."

Collins rose, pitched his meal at the fire, and went for his horse. He mounted and whipped the big red to a gallop. Pryor let him go.

Gibson muttered: "Runnin' the horse in the heat, no good for the both of them."

Pryor turned on Gibson suddenly. "Running like a mad dog at the mouth won't make him better, either, Private. He'll be back. Cap'n says enough for today. We're campin' here tonight."

Wind in his face and ringing in his ears brought relief to John Collins. He tried to decipher words on the wind — like York said, he called and called, but there was never an answer. He rode back into camp after the captain and sergeants had retired and the west wind blew ragged clouds across the moon. The air had cooled. He turned the horse loose by the river, walked to the water, cupped his hands, and splashed his face. It eased the fitful heat of his brain. He dunked his head and felt coolness wash the grit from his hair and glide over his sun-parched neck. Insects of the night called and the buffalo bulls were still roaring after their mates.

After dark, it began to rain in small, sparse droplets, and Collins returned to camp. A few men, unable to sleep, lingered by a low fire that they'd lit to dispel the mosquitoes. They fell silent as Collins walked up. Gibson was right. It had been too long since they'd heard him laugh. He used to laugh, long and loud, with Colter and Labiche and all of them, but the closer he came to the Mandan villages, the more he retreated, and memories got in the way. He stood like a statue and waited. Bratton moved to make space. No one spoke.

He sat down, pulled a worn buffalo skin around his wet shoulders. The rain increased and drops pattered against the dry hide like batons on the stretched skin of a drum. His head throbbed to the rhythm. Men moved away to find shelter, but Collins fell asleep right there, slumped over on the bare earth, and Bratton laid him flat and spread the hide over him.

In the morning, his joints ached, but the rain had stopped. He watched Shannon jog lazily down from the southern hills, shagging an errant horse before him. He should have been with him. Behind Shannon, a thin gray coil twisted into a white fluff of clouds. Collins rubbed his sleepy eyes. As Bratton came, he pointed and mumbled: "Lightning there."

Bratton looked, snapped bolt upright, and cried out with all the power of his lungs: "Fire on the mountain!"

Sergeant Gass screeched only seconds later: "Smoke, south flank. Drive in the tinkering stragglers. Bunch them close."

Collins punched his bedding into a tight roll and scanned the horizon. To the north, an answering column sprouted. He found his voice: "North, more smoke." The entire camp came alive, gathering supplies, saddling and packing horses, gulping whatever breakfast could be swallowed whole. Collins didn't wait for the order. He ran for his horse and raced to join Shannon. They pressed the horses, shoulder to shoulder, and drove them east down the valley of Clark's Fork as the smoke rose on the hillsides to their left, right, and rear. Then it dissipated like giant puffs of Charbonneau's pipe.

In the afternoon, not a cloud marred the cobalt dome of sky. Collins was riding on the herd's far flank when Shannon trotted up beside him. "Ain't seen Injuns since we left the Bone-In-The-Noses. That was no lightning fire, Johnny. That was man-set." Shannon expected a response.

Collins said: "From those hills, Injuns can pick us off like a pigeons on a fence. Wonder who they are. Maybe the hellish Blackfeet are here."

"Then Captain Lewie and Drouillard won't be comin' back." Shannon's face blanched, but Collins only stared at the horses. He was thankful for the danger. It was immediate and compelling and evicted the longing from his heart.

At the nooning, speculation buzzed. Who was the presence that shadowed their trail and lit the fires? Were they Blackfeet, Spanish, British, or some other? Were they friendly or war-like? They did not attack. Perhaps they were too few.

Finally Charbonneau pronounced: "Crows . . . they are Crows." He enunciated so forcefully he nearly spat his pipe from between his teeth. Charbonneau had lived with the Crows, knew their cunning ways, and added: "They are friendly, but they are worse thieves than the river natives, the worst horse thieves on the plains. They are masters of stealth, and on the plains there is no place to hide."

Sergeant Pryor seconded him. "Keep a sharp eye, boys. Could be sniffin' our droppings and we'd never see 'em. Twenty of us, forty eyes." He corrected himself. "Twenty-one well armed."

"An' a woman an' a babe. Injuns won't attack women." Shannon snatched at any shred of hope.

"Blackfeet will. Ask a Shoshone. Ask Charbonneau's wife. They just capture women for slaves."

York blinked when Bratton made the comment.

In less than an hour, they were moving again, guns in hand. Clark led. Steadily, anxiously, two by two, they marched. Seven men bunched the herd tightly between them. Shannon and Pryor, wary, rode the south flank; Charbonneau and York, the north; Patrick Gass, at point. Colter and Collins, side-by-side, choked on dust in the rear. They rode frequent tiny circles to check the country all around. The woman hovered on her pony with her babe behind Captain Clark. The rest of the corps pulled pack horses on tight leads behind. Four more smokes rose to the southeast before a rainstorm spattered the valley. When the clouds separated, light dispersed in a shower of colors that revealed the towering, conical mountains behind them, but not one single smudge of smoke.

Clark's voice blared finally: "Grass an' water ahead! Make camp!" They drove in the horses and dismounted. Collins didn't stay long. Clark himself saw to that. "Eat and ride, Collins, Colter. Shannon and Gibson relieve at midnight, then Bratton and Potts one hour before dawn. I'll join you at dawn. Indians love the dawn."

Collins swallowed his meal, gulped water, and caught the red horse. He mounted and circled the herd, slowly, clockwise. Colter rode counterclockwise and tried to snatch snips of conversation on each lonely go-around. "We'll make it to the old cache tomorrow. Tobacco's in that hole. Smoke in your lungs, Johnny, calm your frazzled nerves."

Collins was in no mood to talk and clamped his lips together in a needle line.

Finally, on the third go-around, Colter surmised: "We raise the boats, don't need horses no more." He didn't expect an answer, but Collins objected with force: "Can't abandon horses. Horses'll buy us more meat an' robes than ten chests of your infernal gold."

Colter grinned and quipped: "That they will, Johnny." He should've stopped there, but he reverted to the prickly talk of last night's fire. "Will they buy me a wife like they bought you yours? Or a cranky mother-in-law? You'd like that, so's you could sick 'er on me, wouldn't you, Johnny?" And he laughed.

Collins jerked his horse's head around and kicked it hard away. The animal squealed in protest. He rode wide on his next rounds and avoided Colter for the rest of the night. Nine horses disappeared on their watch and didn't come back.

On July 8th they arrived at the site of their encampment of last August 17th. The canoes were still sunk in the pond where they'd left them. Men leaped from their horses, scrambled to the tobacco cache, and dug with their bare hands. In minutes, they were unwrapping the first carrot. It had not rotted. It wasn't even damp. Clark who gave a genial nod, sliced off two feet of the braided weed, and tossed it to Bratton who passed it around.

Labiche and Tom Howard raised the dugouts. The only damage was a layer of fine silt. Labiche winked at Collins. "Now I show you how to ride, in a boat. No more horse. I go with Ordway to the Three Forks. You

204

and Clark and your beloved horses, go by land." He winked again, adding: "I wager my boats arrive first to the place where the rivers meet."

Collins took the bet. But Labiche's news gnawed at his heart. The corps was dividing again. Now he was losing Labiche. To face a Blackfoot challenge, there were fewer and fewer — fewer to defend horses and property, fewer to defend life and limb. Collins had a compelling reason to live — to see Laughing Water again. Captain Clark and the sergeants let the parting celebration ring late into the night. But John Collins was fearful and sick.

Next morning at first light, York went to pray as William Clark called a final muster. The corps gathered near the shore, and, when all weapons were inspected and all the baggage packed, Sergeant Ordway shoved off with Labiche and nine others. Collins watched them sail away with a sinking heart. When he and Colter and Shannon rode out to gather the horses, they discovered a discarded quirt and tracks of many hoofs that disappeared where the trail crossed hard rock. They spotted a few horses, two or three at a glance. But these were the stragglers. More of the herd was missing.

John Colter shook his head. "Charbonneau was right. Crows are with us. Means the Blackfeet ain't."

They spread out to find the missing animals. The result, when Collins counted, was frightening.

"Twenty more missing, our best and fastest, and nine of our men are floating happily down the river when we need them here. What was Clark thinking?" Colter only tightened his jaw and gave a hard stare. Collins stroked his horse's proud red neck, muttering: "Trust a horse more than my captain. Like Charbonneau says . . . 'Crows, the best horse thieves on the plains.' They left us the skinny an' lame."

Colter said in disbelief: "Almost half the herd, half of all our wealth gone." He snapped his fingers. "In a heartbeat." Then he winked and stated: "Injuns won't steal gold."

They reported the loss to Captain Clark. A red surge of anger colored Clark's weathered face and the hammering in his cheek drummed. Angrily he griped: "Go after them. Shoot the rascals if you must."

But the Indians and horses had vanished without a trace.

With the remaining horses, they followed the river. The land flattened and the valley spread widely. The expanse of grassland opened like a vast yellow carpet before them and waist-high stalks swayed in a light wind like waves of the sea. Elk and antelope grazed and the buffalo bulls roared. Colter raised his rifle and shot a fat bull.

That night, when they camped, the talk was cheerful until Shannon dared ask: "Wonder how's Lewie?" Immediately the easy banter died. Drouillard, the Fields brothers, Warner, Frazer, Gass, and Captain Lewis, were they alive or dead? No one answered. And what of Labiche and Ordway sailing downriver? They made a tempting target.

Collins felt a knot in the pit of his stomach harden and the bile bubble up in his throat. He coughed, but the cruel plug compressing his burgeoning emotions would not dislodge. He left the fire and walked off into the darkness where the vision of Laughing Water arose in the night sky. He had only known her in the white of winter, and he wondered how she appeared in the bright light of the summer sun. Suddenly the camaraderie of his fellows seemed trivial, and the Crow and Blackfeet threat distant. Thirty or forty miles a day, they were moving quickly now, ever closer to the rendezvous with Lewis, Drouillard, and Labiche, and the earth lodge villages of the Mandans.

A surge of desire made him shudder when he thought of her. Their coupling had been direct and open, without flirtation and dissimilation, like no other in his young experience, until the buffalo ceremony when Mandans shared their women with their bravest and strongest warriors. Even ancient warriors, stomping and huffing like the buffalo bulls they imitated, claimed the right. The ceremony was sacred to the Mandans, but it repelled John Collins. It contradicted the very beliefs in which he had been reared. One ecstatic winter, he'd passed with her. It was not long enough to change his beliefs or hers. They were too deeply imbedded. Yet soon he would arrive at her village. What should he say? Could he snatch the words in Mandan from an imperfect memory? How would she return his greeting? Could he redefine his life to live with her in her village? He returned to camp. The fire had died and the men slept. Exhausted, not from physical effort but from the bitter struggle in his soul, he lay his bed and fell asleep.

A few hours later, in the early dawn, he pulled himself into the saddle. The even stride of the red horse lulled his brain until a shout shook the stillness. Colter's voice, he knew the shriek. "Smoke in the lowlands!" Collins grabbed his rifle. But a cheer broke the clamor, and the youthful voice of Shannon sounded: "It's Labiche and the boats!"

Collins smiled and his tense muscles eased. He'd lost his bet, but his heart was glad. The group had sailed ninety-seven miles the first day, as far as they had ever come in one day. Labiche had reached the forks on the third day, July 12th. Collins, Shannon, and Colter arrived with the horses one day later.

When they approached the fire where Labiche was stirring the pot, Collins grinned and blundered: "You always knew you'd win."

Labiche replied with a laugh: "The river runs faster than a horse can travel. It does not tire and it does not tempt thieves. Eat your soup. Never will I ride another horse for the rest of my life." With a friendly jab in the ribs, he added: "And one day, I find me a long-legged wife like yours."

It was a flip remark, tossed like a handful of dust in the air, but Collins's face contracted in pain and he covered it with his hands.

"Be happy. You found us, and you'll find her." When Collins didn't answer, Labiche added: "God will grant you both many years of happiness. You'll see. She'll be there. The Mandans do not migrate like wild geese. I told York to pray, and Cruzatte, in case God won't

208

listen to an old pirate or a slave. I tell them to pray for you. If you want, I will wager that she is waiting."

Collins grinned at Labiche's smug confidence. He had never associated the worldly pirate with a deity and asked: "You believe in God?"

"Sometimes." Labiche grinned and rubbed the scar on his face. "I am a gambler, Johnny. My French father always told me God is a good bet. Gamble that God is good, that is what I do. I cannot risk life or limb thinking that God is bad and evil holds sway." He laughed and pitched an errant stick into the fire. "You saved Bratt, Johnny. You didn't push him like deadfall over the cliff. You brought him back. We'll bring you back. I'll bring you back. Drouillard will bring Lewis back. And you will see her." He studied Collins's drawn face. "Look at us, a slave, a pirate, a bunch of rowdy tramps that the wind blew together. That's what we are and we've come far. Except Floyd who died."

The next morning, Captain Clark gathered his men. They sat cross-legged or stood slouching over long rifle barrels, but they listened intently to their captain. "Sergeant Ordway will follow the Missouri to the great falls and help McNeal and Goodrich organize the portage. They will raise the *pirogue* and supplies we buried at White Bear Island. The rest of you march to the Yellowstone and explore that river with me. In separate groups, we will advance more quickly toward our rendezvous with Captain Lewis where the Yellowstone River flows into the Missouri." He paused to survey the gaunt, hairy faces of his men and assign each his duty. No one objected, and he concluded: "To each and all, good luck and Godspeed."

Again, Labiche went with Ordway to organize the boats. Collins and Colter stayed behind and accompanied Clark and Sergeant Pryor to the horses. York, the slave, was not permitted a choice.

Collins waved a hand at the departing canoes and watched his friend, Labiche, sail away once more. He stared until he could spot only tiny specks and recalled how the dreadful monster of the Nez Percés had swallowed all living things. The wild river was consuming his companions, and his hopes. He closed his eyes and listened for the wind. There was no sound. Then he remembered how Coyote had outsmarted the monster of the Nez Percé people. Sergeant Pryor was no coyote, but maybe Labiche could be so cunning.

CHAPTER
SEVENTEEN

On July 14th, William Clark, eight men, a woman, and a baby set out across a fertile plain and arrived on the banks of the Yellowstone. Beavers dammed the flow, herons waded in the fish-filled shallows, and tall, conical firs crowned gentle, surrounding hills. The sky shone a deep cobalt blue with an occasional white fluff of cloud blowing swiftly on the west wind. Nearly every evening, a thunder-shower scrubbed the colors of the earth to a polished shine. But available wood was soft, unsuited to dugouts, and the troop started east by pack train. They left the mountains behind and edged their way along high rim rocks that defined the riverbed and gave way to gentle hills. Trees disappeared except for ancient cottonwoods and scrub willow growing in the basin of the river. They made their camps visibly, in the open, where the smoke of Indian fires on the hills at their backs wafted down upon them.

No one dared give vent to fear until the hired scout, Toussaint Charbonneau, accosted the captain. The blackened pipe that he clamped between his teeth and hard French accent slurred most of his speech, but he removed the pipe to lend gravity to his words. "Natives follow us like stalking cats. My wife is afraid because they seized her once. I told her that horses have greater value."

Clark glared from under a wet hide that he had wrapped around his head to foil the mosquitoes. He lived as his men did now, dressed as they dressed, ate when they ate, suffered when they suffered, and feared when they feared. Charbonneau's complaint elicited a chorus of yeas and Clark replied: "We see smoke, not people. We cannot guard against what we cannot see."

Charbonneau bit down on his pipe, inhaled, and blew out a stream of smoke, complaining: "Smoke obscures vision and hides danger. We are too small a force to guard so many horses."

Clark did not blink. He drew back his broad shoulders, met the Frenchman's iron glare, and asserted: "We are nine sure shots . . . force enough." But his head bobbed as if he had not convinced himself and he coughed to free his lungs from the smoke that Charbonneau exhaled.

Then Bratton raised a shaky voice: "Injuns have no guns. They don't steal boats. We'd go more quickly on the crest of the river, in boats."

They took a vote. Captain Clark, York, Charbonneau, Bratton, and Pryor voted for boats, the rest for horses. Compromise came grudgingly. They built two dugouts wide as the diameter of available trees allowed — twenty-eight feet long, eighteen inches deep, and two feet wide. They close-herded the horses. But Crows descended invisibly in the night and stole more horses, among them the big red stud. The two men on guard never heard a sound.

Loss of the horse was another blow to John Collins. The animal had been companion and pet. He was a social young man, had formed loyalties and relationships, and had always relied on the constancy of mentors and friends. Now they were disappearing, and he had eased the separation with an attachment to the horse.

He begged permission to go after the animal, and William Clark acceded. At dawn, he and Colter rode out across a level plain to a place where the trail disappeared into a maze of hard, dry hills. They climbed a steep trail that grew steadily more rocky until hoof prints barely marked the thin soil. When the horses began to lag, Collins pushed on grimly. White beads of sweat pearled the animal's chest, and its breath came labored and loud.

Colter's horse stumbled hard and Colter dismounted and called a halt. "I'm going back," he said, "before I kill this horse or he kills me."

Collins whirled on his companion. "You can't. Without horses we die."

Colter's protest was loud: "Wrong, Johnny . . . without horses, we walk, we sail, we live, if we claw our way back. You don't kill one horse to save another. Could end up killin' 'em both. Injuns got fresh mounts an' they know the trail. Blackfeet, Flatheads, Shoshones, we could be ridin' into a nest of murderers."

Collins drew his lips back tightly against his teeth and scattered his syllables like birdshot. "I gave my word, Colt. I'll kill the rogues that took 'em." He drew his rifle from its sling.

Colter was dismissive. His attitude pricked Collins more. "Put the gun away, Johnny. You want a fancy horse to impress your woman. Don't kill me to do it."

Collins's face blanched. He raised his rifle in a swift half circle until the muzzle pointed at John Colter's heart, but Colter didn't flinch.

Colter looked straight down the barrel of the gun and laughed. "You wouldn't point that gun at me. It ain't loaded, is it? Labiche teach you to bluff? I'm goin' back to grass an' water, an' I'm walkin' this poor animal. Load that gun, Johnny, an', when I turn my back, shoot when you're ready, but don't shoot this innocent animal." He pivoted on his heel and tugged his grateful horse after him.

Collins pulled the trigger. The ball exploded from the barrel in a burst of fire and smoke. It hit the rock surface of the trail and sent shards flying. The noise sent Colter's horse charging down the trail, pulling John Colter with him. They stopped twenty yards on and Colter shot a withering glance at Collins.

Collins lowered his eyes, slung the gun back over his shoulder, and shuddered at the dark impulses of his own heart. He jabbed his heels into his horse and jerked the horse up the trail. It side-stepped and pitched its head, puffed, and pawed forward over loose shale that began to slide. Collins leaped off as the animal skidded, then scrambled its way to solid ground and stood, trembling with fright. Blood oozed from a gash in its right front knee.

Colter smirked and remonstrated: "Now you've lamed the beast. Think you can catch an Indian on foot?"

Collins compressed the budding anger in his chest, picked up the reins, and started down behind Colter. Brooding resentment settled on his heart like a cold, wet cloak.

When they came to a meadow where a cold spring gushed, Colter stopped to let his horse drink. Collins bathed his horse's wound. Neither man spoke for the duration of the trip back to camp. They arrived without the stolen horses, without even a beaver or grouse for dinner.

Colter related the incident to Sergeant Pryor. "Don' know what come over 'im, sir. He misses Drouillard an' that ugly pirate, Labiche. Mention that Injun woman he married an' he goes crazy. He raised 'is gun at me who's his friend, an' he fired. Didn't mutter one lousy word all the way home. Like he's got wind in 'is ears an' in 'is head. He ain't sorry, no, sir."

Pryor ran his fingers through his beard. "What do you want me to do with him?"

"Keep him in camp, sir, with folks. Watch 'im."

"And if he won't stay?"

"He'll stay. He'll sulk, but he'll stay."

When Collins heard of his confinement, he made a lonely bed in a dark clump of spruces. At dawn, when York went to pray, he tripped over his sleeping form. Instinctively Collins snapped his knees to his chest and kicked with all his force. York jumped back, and Collins glared at the wary white eyes in the dark face as if they

215

were a wooden mask. The slave left, said his prayer, and returned and helped Collins rise, then led him to the fire.

After breakfast, Clark called the tiny group together and outlined his plan. "Sergeant Pryor, Privates Shannon, Windsor, and Hall drive the remaining horses overland to the mouth of the Bighorn, then strike overland to the Mandan villages. The rest of you . . . Collins, Colter, Bratton, Mister Charbonneau and his woman and babe, accompany me to the rendezvous with Captain Lewis at the mouth of the Yellowstone." He fell silent, as had become his habit, awaiting comment from his men.

Bratton raised his gentle voice: "Four o' them, six o' us if the Injun woman can shoot, all easy targets."

Collins protested: "We are too small a force to resist an attack."

Colter disagreed: "Four's all there were when we met the Shoshones."

"You're all bluster, Colt. Twenty-five able men, twenty-five sure shots met the Shoshones."

"And you're a damned coward, Collins, scared to face a couple o' Crows. You aimed a gun at me, one of your friends, because you knew I wouldn't fight."

Collins eyes and lips narrowed. Raw anger creased his handsome face.

Bratton stepped gingerly between the two. Collins diverted his gaze to the river flowing swiftly by. A cold wind struck him across the eyes. He breathed deeply and tried to calm. Emotions welled up and conflicted. The need to justify himself finally exploded in harmless speech. "What am I doing? What are you doing, Colt? Why are we . . . all of us here? Lewis and Drouillard and a pitiful few go to confront the entire Blackfeet nation. Pryor, with three men, trails a herd that needs ten men to guard them. The Crows can send forty men to drive them away. Thompson, Warner, and McNeal must complete a portage that took thirty men sixteen days. Ordway will arrive late to help, if he gets there at all. And we seven who are left squat in two hollow sticks you call boats. We have no guide. We follow no known trail. Falls, rapids, tribes who steal and plunder, what else will we face?" He closed his eyes and pinched the eyelids, expecting a rebuke from his captain.

William Clark replied softly: "Is that all, Private Collins? I see a brighter future than you. I pray that you, that we all will live to enjoy the bright prairie sky."

Seconds of quiet intervened before Bratton murmured softly: "We could lash two dugouts together, sir. Two would be more stable than one and proceed as quickly."

William Clark smiled and replied: "Good, Private Bratton. See to it. Collins, come with me."

On July 24th, when the morning sun was high, Collins watched the four men drive the horses across the river and set out over the plain. Dust settled in their wake as he shoved off into the flooding Yellowstone and felt the current seize the little boat. It propelled them ninety long miles past foothills and benches and through cañons carved by centuries of flowing water. They came ashore where a huge profusion of sandstone, 200 feet high, commanded the river. Images of buffalo, antelope, figures that a human hand had carved, scarred its craggy face. They climbed the rock that they baptized Pompey's Tower after Charbonneau's infant son, and looked back where they had come. Then they turned their gaze east over the wide, empty plain.

Collins gave only a cursory glance, shuddered, then scrambled like a spider back down to the river. There he sat huddled in a tight ball when the others returned. Bratton found him and lay a soothing hand upon his shoulder. He sat and listened as John Collins raved. "Scratch some letters that they can't read, that I can't read, that nobody will ever read. Why?"

"We're smarter than that, Johnny."

"Smart? Not smart enough to cure you."

"You pulled me outta the hole yourself, Johnny."

Collins shook his head. "Nez Percé dug that hole, told us how deep an' how wide. They saved you, Bratt."

"Not the way I see it. I owe you, Johnny. Like Labiche promised, we're bringin' you back. If he don't come back, I'll watch out for you, make a smithy o' you yet." He rambled on about life and love and friendship and loneliness. When they made camp, Bratton made him eat, set out his bedding, and lay him down. After Collins fell asleep, Bratton explained to Colter: "He loves that heathen wife o' his. He won't feel better till he sees her an' he can make it right. Left her under a curse, an' the curse gets heavier the closer we come back."

Colter was incredulous. "A woman cursed him, made him threaten me? He believes in curses?"

Bratton nodded. "Don't matter if he believes. Maybe it already worked its evil. Like York says, an evil wind. We've seen stranger things on this trip."

They slept, and soon the morning came. It was time to leave. When William Clark issued the order, Bratton came for Collins. But Collins wouldn't move, and Clark had to grab him by the back of his shirt and jerk him to his feet. "I have to carry you, Private?" He shoved a paddle in Collins's hand and commanded: "Row." Mechanically John Collins climbed aboard and dipped the paddle.

CHAPTER
EIGHTEEN

Days were sunny, nights warm, and game plentiful. They stayed late on the Yellowstone where a light breeze was welcome and waterfowl honked in the cool of the evening. Collins rowed and the canoe sped swiftly downriver over the smooth surface of water. In camp, he huddled with the other six in the path of the fire's smoke, because smoke repelled the insects that landed on every surface of exposed skin.

In seven short days, they sighted the churning of waters where the Yellowstone flows into the wide Missouri and, on August 3rd, they arrived at the rendezvous. The shore rose gently from a copse of cottonwoods to a treeless plain that stretched farther than the eye could see. They marched up the gentle rise and let their eyes gloat on the vastness. Grasses waved in a soft wind all the way to the horizon. Buffalo, elk, and antelope grazed. A hawk circled, then dived for its meal. But of man, Indian or white, Captain Lewis, Sergeant Ordway, Georges Drouillard, and the other loyal men of the Corps of Discovery, there was no sign.

Collins made a lonely bed and awakened with eyes that opened to thin slits.

Bratton was standing over him. "Mosquitoes made a meal o' you." He held out a wet cloth. "Hold this on yer face. Keep it wet. We're movin' to higher ground."

They left only a note, telltale footprints, and the ashes of last night's fire, and then marched to the summit of a hill where the cool prairie wind drove off the mosquitoes. Another day passed. No one arrived.

On the third day, at breakfast, the little group sat together in the thick smoke of a blazing fire. Bratton coughed and muttered: "Should've waited for Cap'n Lewie where we said we would." He set down two bucketfuls of water that he'd hauled up the hill from the river. Charbonneau shaded his eyes from the blistering sun and squinted steadily at the river.

Collins dipped his tin cup, sipped, and mumbled: "Maybe we're all that's left. Maybe Blackfeet got 'em. Maybe bears or snakes or wolves or the river. Maybe they drowned."

Charbonneau mouthed his pipe. "Drouillard's with Lewis. Drouillard's a good scout."

Colter added: "Blackfeet's like mosquitoes. They like blood." He laughed and slapped his cheek. "Blackfeet an' bugs buzz thicker than old Delashelwilt's whores."

They kept the fire blazing on a high bluff overlooking the river to signal Lewis and the others. The billowing smoke could be seen upriver and down and over the surrounding plain. But Lewis did not arrive.

To escape the swarming bugs, they moved farther down the Missouri, farther from the assigned meeting place at the mouth of the Yellowstone. Each day, despite the heat, a hot fire burned. They hunted, butchered, preserved meat, hauled water, prepared hides, and filled the endless, worrisome hours with chatter. Clark rotated the watch day and night and spent hours combing the shore for evidence of Lewis. The silence, that had blighted Collins's days on the river, descended on each and every man as anxiety for their fellows mounted with every passing hour.

August 8th, at noon, they ate a mournful meal. The boat rested in the shallows. Assigned to look-out, Collins ate a spare meal, climbed the high rock, and trained the spyglass on the river. A momentary shadow flicked off the silvery rocks and hovered in the moist air that rose off the water. He aimed the glass, adjusted the lens, and recognized a round, bobbing bullboat. Waving both arms, he screamed: "Boat, Indians comin' down!"

Four men threw down bowls and ran for rifles. Clark scaled the rocks to Collins's perch, grabbed the glass, focused, and shouted fearful, fractured orders. "Mister Charbonneau, take rifles, guard the dugout. Colter, put out the fire. Take cover. Where's Bratton?" He let the glass fall, and stopped to load his rifle.

Collins answered: "Hunting, sir. Dugout's well hidden, sir." He picked up the glass and looked again: "Two boats, not one, sir."

Collins trained the glass on the twin brown blots in the river. They moved closer now, their dark hazy outlines assuming shape and definition. "Movin' to our side of the river, sir. Two men in each boat, sir." His next words shattered like splintered glass. "Armed, sir, with rifles."

222

William Clark gazed down on the tiny group gathered at the dying fire. They were all who were left — Charbonneau, Collins, Colter, himself, and Bratton, if Bratton returned. Here was the last ragged remnant of the forty-two men who'd left St. Louis — plus one slave, one Indian woman, and one child. Clark muttered: "Pray, Private, that they pass on by. Prepare to defend." He repeated the last words loudly, and raised the glass to his eye once again. A mosquito had settled on the lens. Impatiently he crushed the insect with his thumb, and blood from its engorged body oozed over the lens. Clark threw down the instrument and wiped his bloody finger frantically against his tunic. He stood glaring at the approaching boats, lips moving as if to speak, but no sound came.

Collins sensed his fear, the same that swelled in his own soul, and picked up the glass with trembling hands. It had not broken. He wiped the red smear from the lens.

Colter climbed up beside him and held out a hand for the glass, muttering: "See the field of fire like a hawk from up here." Colter had excellent vision, second only to Drouillard's.

Collins handed him the glass, muttering: "They are four. We are five." He passed the glass to Colter, who scanned the shoreline and murmured: "Where's York?" York had vanished from sight. Immobile and silent, William Clark stood on the outcrop. The bullboats came on. Bratton arrived from the hunt, joined them.

The man in the first boat fired into the air and the loud report echoed across the river.

Bratton's voice shook as he murmured: "Injuns with guns." The furrows in his brow deepened and he added: "Got Lewis an' they're comin' for us."

But the same man lay down his gun and paddled furiously toward the near shore. York appeared, running up the beach, feet splattering the watery gravel, waving his rifle frantically. Colter griped: "Fool slave, tell ever'body we're here."

But York's strident voice filled the air. "Friends, massa, friends, Pryor, Hall, Windsor, and Shannon."

Colter clapped a hand to his mouth in disbelief, then thumped Collins on the back so hard he coughed. "You hear, Johnny, more of our own, alive."

Collins shook his head in disbelief. "But they went overland with the horses."

Captain Clark closed his eyes and let out an audible sigh. The tension in his tall frame melted, and he fell to sitting cross-legged, hugging himself and rocking to and fro.

Collins turned a wan face toward his captain and muttered: "Pryor's comin', sir, without horses, but he's comin'."

Clark whispered — "Thanks be to God." — and wiped away a tear. He rose and his blue eyes engulfed the four ragged figures splashing through the shallows. He said: "Horses, Private, are the least of our worries."

The welcome was warm, but Pryor shook his head ruefully when he related the loss of the horses. "We hobbled the worst wanderers, sir, bedded them on good grass so they could graze. I'm sorry." His voice croaked. He looked away and Shannon continued: "Sergeant blames hisself, sir, but four men weren't enough to close herd thirty head, day an' night, an' keep 'em fed with Injuns all around, sniffin' like hounds on 'coon scent. We were tired, sir. They came at night, loosed the hobbles, an' started 'em runnin' before we'd even grabbed a rifle. Never heard a sound or saw a flicker till they was poundin' turf an' gallopin' away. Popped off a shot at some ghost in the dark. No moon. Didn't want to hit a horse. Couldn't see. By the time I reloaded, they were gone."

Pryor added: "Like Charbonneau says, Crows are the wiliest horse thieves I ever saw. No way we could chase 'em on foot in the dark or track 'em come mornin'."

Colter mumbled: "We were seven. Add four, makes eleven. If Shields and Gibson make it back . . . thirteen. Count the woman . . . fourteen." He winked. "Twice what we were yesterday, Johnny."

Three more days passed. They moved downriver a few miles each day, and at each campsite built a signal fire and left sign. On the third morning, August 11th, the joy of reunion had passed and they set sail early. Sergeant Pryor sat in the bow of the lead boat, held the glass, and called suddenly: "Dugout beached in willows at two o'clock!" He looked again and shouted: "White men sure as my blood's red!"

The newcomers were Handcock and Dickson, trappers on their way upriver, and they brought news from St. Louis, the first the corps had heard since they'd left the last white settlement of La Charette, over two years before. James Madison was the new President and settlers by the hundreds were floating down the Ohio, crossing the Mississippi, populating Louisiana. The Mandans were fighting the Minnetarees and the Assiniboins were killing North West traders. The Sioux, toll keepers of the river, were active as always and had robbed these two trappers of all they possessed. Handcock and Dickson listened eagerly to every word of advice from the corps until Colter interjected: "Blackfeet're worse than Sioux. They'll suck your blood an' spit it out."

Unimpressed, Handcock countered: "You ever met a Blackfoot?"

Colter blared back: "No, but our fellows went to find them and haven't come back. We all heard the stories from Shoshones, Flatheads, Nez Percés."

Silence fell like cold rain.

The morning of August 12th dawned red and windy. Collins awakened to the hum of York praying. The slave's voice was lower now. He no longer knelt but sat on a convenient log and murmured his litany. Soon, they shoved off once more toward the bloody rays of the rising sun in two dugouts and two bullboats.

They had not gone far when young Shannon clapped a hand to his side. "Tomahawk's gone, back at last night's camp. I remember where I left it." Red-faced, he stammered an explanation to avoid blame. "I was flakin' wood. Chips burn brighter, so's Lewie an' the rest are sure to find us."

Pryor did not mince words. "Leave it. Lewis will know we were there and bring it on for you."

But Clark sent Shannon back for the weapon. Hall and Gibson went hunting, and the rest waited. The hours slowed to a trickle as the heat of the day increased.

"Shannon's takin' too long. Can't find his hatchet. He's lost." Colter volunteered to go after him, but Clark refused.

It began to rain hot pelting blobs of moisture. They chewed cold meat and glared at rocks, grass, anything to evade looking another man in the eye and avoid acknowledging how vulnerable they were. Shannon did not return. A light breeze arose and blew the cooling rain off. Bratton rose to stretch his legs. Colter tossed stones in the river. Suddenly he raised an arm and stopped in mid-throw. "I don't believe it."

Three pinpoints of black sailed out from the shadows of the rain clouds into the brilliant sunshine. A *pirogue* and two dugouts approached from upriver. No one could mistake Georges Drouillard's bellow: "Halo the camp, *mes amis*, my friends!"

The waiting men charged toward the shore in a cheering, whooping mass. They waded out to meet the arriving boats, seized bowlines, and tugged the boats up the beach. The men in the boats jumped out, swam to shore. Drouillard, Labiche, Ordway, Whitehouse, they were all there. They had raised the cache on White Bear Island and brought clothing, tobacco, an anvil, pots, needles and knives, powder and lead. They hugged, slapped backs, and shrieked for joy. The Corps of Discovery was complete again — except for Captain

Lewis who lay on his stomach, motionless, in the *pirogue*.

Drouillard held the *pirogue* in place against the current and called to Captain Clark as Collins and Bratton strode up to relieve him.

Lewis lay in the hull with a gunshot wound in the back of his thigh and his eyes were glazed over with pain. York carried Meriwether Lewis ashore.

Clark shouted: "Kindle a fire!" Then he questioned: "Assiniboins? Blackfeet? Who did this, Meri?"

"An awful mistake, Will, no Indian."

They laid him, face down, in the shade beneath a tall cottonwood. Clark uncovered a gaping gash in his haunch, three inches deep. It was red, inflamed, threatening. Clark's eyes narrowed to slits as a rush of anger froze his square jaw, He muttered: "Who, Meri? When?"

Lewis heaved himself up on two elbows and began to talk. "We found Blackfeet, Will. Rather they found us, ate with us, slept with us. Like Judases, they betrayed us. Stole our rifles as we slept. Drouillard caught one, grabbed his rifle. The rascal let it go. Joe Fields stabbed another, a gut wound. I think he died." When he paused, Clark did not interrupt. Simple words seemed to relieve his pain. "I shot one, Will, in the belly, killed him. First man I killed in two years on the trail." He shook his head as if to banish the image, and his glassy, grief stricken eyes sought out William Clark as he resumed. "He was stealing horses, robbing our only means of escape, Will. We stopped them, jumped on the horses, and rode for our lives. When we reached the

Missouri, Ordway was passing with the canoes. Turned the horses loose, jumped in, and here we are. Bless John Ordway. He saved our lives." He closed his eyes and punctuated the description with a loud sigh.

Clark drew his thick brows together and pressed his question again: "Who shot you, Meri? That's a dangerous wound."

Lewis turned onto his good hip and winced. "Not as dangerous as painful, Will. I told you, friendly fire . . . a flesh wound. It'll heal." He forced a smile: "I couldn't send word to Bighorn. Blackfeet will continue preying on his people, and his couriers will wait in vain. But he was right, Will. The Blackfeet are a greedy, murdering race. The Nez Percés, the Shoshones, and the Flatheads cannot hunt safely east of the mountains."

Clark was losing patience. Doggedly he repeated: "Meri, who shot you?"

Lewis paused, looked away, then finally admitted: "Cruzatte, old blind beggar, thought I was an elk." He turned his face to the side, collapsed his elbows, and lay flat. Clark's jaw tightened visibly as Lewis added: "Don't condemn him, Will. The man can't see. He has concealed his deteriorating vision from the rest of us. He fears blindness more than death itself. That is punishment enough."

"Can he steer a boat?"

"He can paddle. He cannot navigate."

William Clark grimaced and replied: "The wound is draining. We'll be with the Mandans soon. We can regroup, you can recuperate there."

Lewis nodded wanly. His wound lay open for all to see, but he was too exhausted and pained to care. Clark cleaned the wound and let Lewis sleep.

With their captain injured, speculation began to mushroom like yeast in the sun. Labiche initiated it: "That we'll be in Saint Louis in September, who bets?"

Bratton answered the challenge: "If the Sioux and the Arikaras an' the greedy Brits don't stop us and demand bribes, I say October, pirate." Bratton added wistfully: "Although I might consider stayin' with the Mandans, if Johnny stays. Whaddaya say, Johnny?" Before Collins could answer, Bratton exclaimed: "Well, look who's here!"

George Shannon had returned with his tomahawk. Thankful for the reprieve, Collins smiled because the corps was complete again. But he knew that they could not delay with the Mandans, that they must speed south before word of their coming reached the Sioux and their British allies threw up barriers on the river. He placed his bet with Labiche, but he was hoping to lose.

CHAPTER
NINETEEN

"Colter's not comin' back with the rest of us, Johnny. He's goin' upriver with Dickson and Handcock. You could make your base Matootonha, work with him, an' stay with your pretty wife." The statement spilled amicably from the lips of gentle Joe Whitehouse, but it hit Collins like the broadside of an axe. Whitehouse sat with Bratton, Labiche, Drouillard, and Collins. He sewed moccasins while Labiche honed knives, Bratton and Collins cooked, and Drouillard tamped tobacco into the bowl of a pipe. Whitehouse had been absent with Lewis for the last month and was spiking chunks of meat into his mouth with the point of his awl. He chewed while he sewed and didn't notice the gawks of his messmates. Without looking up, he added: "Good-lookin' woman, that wife o' yours."

Collins didn't mince words. "Joe, she threw me out."

Whitehouse shrugged. "One old lady scotched you, not the girl."

Memories of Laughing Water, vivid, compelling, and beautiful, flooded back. Her graceful gait and lithe form were lovely even bundled in buffalo skins in the snow. Her eyes glowed in the light of the lodge fire bright as flashes of sun on glittering snow. The scent of her, the smoothness of her cheek, her touch beneath the robes, the loving smile that beamed up at him when the buffalo drums pounded, he could see it all. But his thoughts turned inevitably to the strange fertility ritual intended to give strength and courage to Mandan infants yet unborn. She was suddenly living, breathing, pressed against him in the crowded ceremonial lodge, and he was shielding her from the lewd advances of another, older and uglier, and then fleeing with her down the snowbound trail to his humble quarters behind the gates of Fort Mandan. Joseph Whitehouse was part of that memory. He'd been sleeping in a dark bunk when Collins entered with Laughing Water. He had awakened, when he heard them talk, and sat up. Laughing Water had seen only his hulking black silhouette that rose like the Mandan devil god seeking vengeance. She had shrieked and fled in panic.

Now Collins shrank from Whitehouse's glance. He set down his bowl and moved off. But there was no place to hide.

Whitehouse looked to Labiche for explanation. "I thought Stands In The River set Johnny's problems to right?" Stands In The River was Laughing Water's brother.

Labiche drew a knife across the whetstone and replied: "Stands In The River apologized, but there was no reconciliation. Johnny never saw her again and he couldn't erase the old lady's curse."

"What curse? She's his wife."

Labiche let cynicism taint his reply. "Life will cheat a man worse than dice or nimble fingers, and reward the undeserving. The grandmother cursed and banished him. Who knows what she'll do when he returns?" The blade whistled and tortured the eardrums as it scraped the whetstone. Labiche waited, then resumed: "What man, white or red, can explain a woman's preference? Look at Charbonneau, the flat-footed lecher. No white woman would want him, yet with the Hidatsas he's married three times."

"Johnny had a better wife than all three."

"He paid a high price. He aimed too high." Labiche remembered he had won the many horses Collins had used for payment.

Labiche and Drouillard went after Collins and led him back to the company. Labiche prompted: "Johnny, Laughing Water has never denied you."

And Drouillard promised: "A year has passed. Stands In The River will have removed the curse." He laughed lightly. "I wager one buffalo robe that she loves you still, *mon ami*, that she is waiting."

Labiche added: "I bet my best knife, and I do not bet it lightly. Trust that she is waiting, *mon ami*."

Colter and Bratton contested the wager more to cheer Collins than to accumulate winnings. The effort succeeded, and Collins's spirits lifted because Labiche and Drouillard were both half Indian and claimed understanding of the peculiar customs of the Mandans.

The wager became the talk of the camp. They were only a few days away from the comfortable Mandan villages and the proximity of the female sex and the men's lust ignited and flamed. Eagerly they trimmed beards, shaved faces, brushed and sewed their tattered clothing, and hoped they each could find a mate as lovely as Collins's wife. It had been a long, lonely trip.

August 14th they beached at Rooptahe, the first of three Mandan villages. Indians rushed to greet them. Black Cat, the village chief, dispatched couriers to Matootonha and Awatixa and the neighboring Hidatsa villages.

In the morning, they sailed on to Matootonha, a commercial hub and veritable maven of earth lodges and home to Laughing Water. The city stood on a high bluff overlooking the river. A stockade surrounded it and a wide moat protected its landward flank. It was midsummer and Indians from numerous tribes gathered in the cool shadow of the ramparts. They came with horses and furs that they traded for corn and beans and the magical metal wares that the white man brought. But most of the permanent residents had decamped to temporary, cooler, summer dwellings among the shady cottonwoods and box elders of the river bottom nearby.

A great clamor greeted the corps at Matootonha. The Mandans splashed into the shallows, hauled in the boats, grasped hands, and clapped shoulders of friends they'd thought were lost. Young and old, warriors, maidens, laughing children, and cranky grandmothers came to welcome the daring men who had braved high mountains, tasted the salty waters of the western sea, and returned to tell the tale. They believed they could acquire the courage, stamina, fabulous weaponry, and magical power of writing by bathing in the breath and basking in the vision of these brave white ones. As

234

a result they plucked hairs from heads, tore scraps from shirts and leggings, scraped the dust from the prints of their moccasins.

Charbonneau's first wife arrived with the first wave of admirers and evoked hoots of derision from the corps who had become attached to Sacagawea and her babe. John Colter led the chorus, yelling: "Sell her, Charbonneau, for what you paid! Sell 'er for gold!"

Charbonneau removed his pipe, lay hold of her arm, and smacked her across the mouth with the back of his hand. They laughed heartily and the woman fled.

The episode in its cruel irony intensified Collins's desire. Where was Laughing Water? He willed her to come for him with the same eagerness the slut had exhibited for flat-footed Charbonneau. But she did not come, and loneliness, like a poisonous tide, washed over him. He admitted to Bratton: "Like you in the ocean, I'm drowning."

Bratton didn't help. He prodded: "You'll see her soon, Johnny?"

Collins shook his head. Aimlessly he wandered among the summer lodges, past scaffolds of drying meat, baskets of vegetables, skins stretched for tanning, and dozens of smiling Indian faces. His eyes scanned each one for her liquid eyes, her welcoming smile. He studied every human movement and posture for the flow of her walk or the tilt of her shoulders. He formed her name in Mandan on his lips, called it aloud, whispered the question to each passer-by: "Where is Laughing Water?" Had he phrased it right, pronounced it correctly? In one year's absence, he'd forgotten so many words. People held their eyes down and walked on by, and the sound of his voice faded somewhere on the breezy wings of the summer wind that blew between the tight clutch of earth lodges.

Finally he found a flat rock near the river, sat, and glared, unblinking, at the passing waters. Tears welled up from the great hollow in his breast. If only time and the river could run backwards. If only he could unravel the horrific buffalo dance. A cold wind picked up and he shivered from the blast. Colder winds had howled during that wondrous winter when he had shared her bed. Then he'd ignored the cold because it harbingered the warmth and life and love in the lodge. But this summer wind chilled the very marrow of his bones. It didn't whisper. It mourned and enfolded the certainty that here on the northern plains, the dead season came early and the time for loving was dreadfully short. He threw a stone in the water and watched it sink.

Drouillard came and knelt beside him. His black, hooded eyes glared at the same water passing. He threw a stick in the water and watched it float downstream. Then he tugged Collins's sleeve and whispered: "Bratton and I were looking for you. Like that stick, *mon ami*, for two years, you've moved with the waters and remained afloat. You will not sink now." He paused to allow Collins to digest the meaning, then added: "While the sun still shines, come, *mon ami*, I know where she is. Sergeant Pryor and the captains give you leave. We go to the old lodge in the city on the bluff."

Hope sparked briefly in Collins's young breast. The old lodge was her winter home, had been their home.

236

Laughing Water must be waiting in the very place where he had left her over one year ago. He grabbed his pack and his rifle and followed Drouillard up the steep switchback path to the permanent village of empty winter lodges. As they climbed, the cold wind blew harder. A cluster of women, who'd been tending their patches of corn and squash, clattered past on their way down, ahead of an approaching storm. The high, playful notes of their chatter rang with the happy clack of their wooden rakes and hoes.

Then the human sounds faded and fell silent and the wind increased. Collins and Drouillard crossed the berm that spanned the wind-tortured water of the moat and passed through a shadowy cut in the earthen walls to the central square. The sacred cedar post stood like a lonely sentinel. Weeds poked their scraggly stalks along the cracked soil of the pathway to the giant ceremonial lodge. The brown earthen humps of lodges seemed humble and dirty now compared with the white purity of the winter scene as Collins remembered it.

Drouillard turned left to the second lodge in the second tier, and stopped. A tall man, still and dignified, stood at the entry. Stands In The River, brother to Laughing Water, nodded a solemn greeting, pushed aside the skin flap that covered the entry, and walked inside.

Collins was about to rush after him, but Drouillard held him back. "Walk softly. Listen quietly with patience and respect. Propriety demands it of you."

The wind lifted the entry's flap as Collins stooped to enter. The interior was dim, the fire ring cold. The underground cellar where the family stored the vegetables lay open and empty. No soft robes graced the sleeping niches, no medicine bundle hung on the windbreak fronting the entry, and only thin needles of light crept feebly through the circular smoke hole in the roof. Slowly Collins circled the lodge as memories flooded back. Foreboding, like an icy needle, pricked at his heart as Stands In The River motioned him to sit in the place of honor in front of the medicine bundle. Drouillard remained standing while the Indian sat opposite and began to speak. Collins strained to grasp the meaning. The language that he'd understood so spontaneously when it had passed her lips seemed harsh and alien now. Stands In The River cast his eyes down at the dry ashes of last winter's fire. Words spilled like stale pits from his mouth without explanatory gesture or expression. They sounded ominous, and Collins willed them to shrivel with the ash in the pit.

Stands In The River fell silent suddenly and pulled a parfleche from his shoulder. He drew out a tiny package wrapped carefully in purest white doeskin. Reverently he laid back the folds in the palm of his hand. There was a thin braid of black hair, smooth as the richest strands of silk. A smaller, finer lock lay unbraided beside it.

Collins muttered incredulously: "Laughing Water's?"

The Indian nodded. He refolded the skin and held it out to Collins.

Collins shook his head wildly in stark denial. He stammered: "She would not cut her hair except for a death." Mandan women sliced off a finger's joint or a lock of hair when a loved one died. It was a common Indian custom.

Stands In The River pressed the bundle gently into Collins's hands as Drouillard explained: "She mourned for you when you went away. For her, it was as if you had died. The grandmother would not let her cut a finger, so she cut her hair to mark her grief."

"But I've returned?" The high pitch of Collins's voice and the intensity of his gaze belied the inevitable. Finally he whispered: "Where is she?"

The silence that followed shattered his last shred of resistance and he understood. His heart was cold, the words frozen in his throat, and he could not voice the sorrow in his soul. He scrambled frantically to his feet.

Drouillard arose with him, blocked the exit, and, gripping his shoulders in his massive fists, he held him in place. He said: "He is not finished. You must sit and listen more, *mon ami*."

Stands In The River raised his voice. "She died giving birth during the freezing moon. She struggled. The baby would not come."

Drouillard added: "The braid is hers, the small lock is the child's."

Collins sat. All at once the earthen interior of the lodge closed in like a dreadful tomb. Collins's body went stiff and he closed his eyes as if to shut it out. But the droning voices of Drouillard and the Indian filled the earthen cavern like vultures' wails, and Drouillard was muttering softly: "The child was yours."

And Stands In The River tried vainly to sooth and explain. "The curse of the grandmother that caused you to flee was not for you. It was she who offended the spirits of her ancestors, not you. They were not yours to offend." He held up a hand. The last small finger was missing and he uttered: "I, too, have suffered."

Tears pressed at the backs of Collins's eyes, but he would not let them spill. He asked: "And the child?"

"A boy. He did not live." Stands In The River turned and pushed Collins and Drouillard ahead of him out through the narrow entryway.

Collins was glad to leave. When they stood in the sunlight again, he asked woodenly: "What of the grandmother?"

"She could not endure her granddaughter's disgrace. The evil consumed her, too."

They stood silently for a long while, three men with heads bowed, each grieving in his way, after his own customs. Collins's tears flowed in silence. Finally Drouillard whispered: "Stands In The River will take us to the resting place, if it will ease your heart."

Collins nodded. It was not far. On the plain behind the village, Laughing Water lay stretched on a high scaffold. The snow, the rain, the burning sun, carrion birds, and the stiff prairie wind had wrought their gruesome work. Shreds of decaying buckskin wrapping hung loosely and blew in a gentle breeze where the flesh had fallen away. Only pieces of her skeleton and matted tufts of hair remained. Of the child, there was only a bone or two.

Collins knelt according to the Catholic custom of his parents, a practice he would have relinquished willingly for her, but which he clung to now, and Drouillard knelt at his side. Together, they made the sign of the cross and intoned the Lord's Prayer. It seemed proper, and he remembered most of the words. Stands In The River did not interrupt. Collins picked up a pebble and caressed it in the crease of his palm. It was red-brown and silken to the touch, cool as her cheek, soft as the strands of her hair, so smooth it felt wet.

Drouillard broke the stillness: "It is rare flint found only here by the rivers, like her. She would have used such a flint to cut her hair." There was no more to say. They left him, and he lingered there. The skies opened and rain poured down. He was glad for the rain because it was cold like his heart and it masked his tears and washed the dust from his hair.

Slowly a great calm settled in his soul. The tears dried and his breathing steadied. He put a hand to his thigh, felt the sheath that housed the pirate's knife whose hilt held the precious stone the color of the sky. He kept it razor-sharp because Labiche had given it to him and prescribed its meticulous care. Drouillard had suggested he give it to Laughing Water as a token of reconciliation. He withdrew the knife, pulled a lock of wet hair away from his scalp, and sliced it off. Carefully he coiled the strands around a joint of his finger. When it was tightly wrapped, he lay his tomahawk flat on the ground, spread the finger upon it, took the knife, and cut off the finger at the first joint. He screamed at the pain. Then he let his blood, like the rain and the river, flow into the ground. He placed the knife, finger, and yellow coil of his hair upon the scaffold. The rain stopped when the wind came up and blew away the clouds. Gradually physical pain replaced the emotional ache.

Drouillard heard his cry, came for him, cut the thong that held the bear's trophies from his neck and bound it tightly around his finger to stop the blood's flow. He spread a robe over Collins's shoulders and spoke gently: "I wagered this robe that she loved you still. Bratton won it and wanted you to have it." He added gravely: "When all the flesh is gone, Stands In The River wants you to know that they will bury her bones with honor."

He led Collins back from the plain, through the deserted village, and down the trail to the camp by the river. Collins followed docilely. Bratton, Shannon, and Colter made a place for him at the fire. Labiche had spitted a beavertail that he'd pegged in the ground to roast. It was Collins's favorite food. Juicy fat dripped from the hot meat, and Labiche picked it up and handed it to Collins. "It will warm you, eat." And Drouillard repeated: "Eat. She would have wanted it. The journey is ending, but not your life."

Collins ate. He was glad to be back among friends. When the rain stopped, he handed the robe back to Bratton, but Bratton refused saying: "It has the stench of death. Burn it." Collins laid it on the fire.

Even Lewis's pained eyes seemed to realize the finality of their days with the Mandans, and the next day, August 16th, they prepared to leave. For those who had formed deep attachments with the Mandan people, and for Lewis who had only begun to recuperate, the visit was too short. But Collins couldn't get away fast enough. They were going home, wherever and whatever that meant. Tomorrow they would begin the final trek. They would ride the flood downriver and hoist the sail with the wind at their backs. They had traveled the route before, and knew where to expect bars and berms and caving banks, hostile tribes, and the opposition of jealous traders. The west wind would compound their speed.

One by one, men began to contemplate a future. Colter tried to tempt John Collins: "Come with me, Johnny, trap furs, find gold, see the earth that smokes like a chimney and gushes steaming water spouts high as the clouds." They had only just heard the fantastic tales from the natives. Collins only shrugged. Colter believed every word.

Charbonneau was staying with the Mandans as factor for the American trade and invited him to stay. Collins refused summarily. Memories were too raw. Labiche wanted to farm, live on solid land in a permanent place. He made no offer, but commiserated: "Fate, Johnny, has not treated you kindly, but it will turn. It always does. Yours is not the only loss. Bratt is too weak to smithy and Cruzatte is going blind. Our captain may walk with a cane. They will find their way and so will you. We all lose and we all win." He added with a wry smile: "I wonder what has become of La Bourgeron, the one you left in Saint Louis? If the old one has died, she is probably rich, but you would not want her back. Maybe I take her."

Collins smiled and rolled his eyes at that. La Bourgeron, née Louise, had pursued him relentlessly.

From the opposite side of the circle, Drouillard mused: "That one is more trouble than all the daughters of Delashelwilt. It would take a pirate to tame her." Drouillard was the last to offer. "I'll stay with the captains, collect my pay. I gave my word. You, too, *mon ami*, you contracted for the duration. Finish with the captains and come with me to the Tennessee and see my Shawnee mother before she dies. Maybe she has a wife for me. Maybe one for you. Maybe not. But she will have comfort and forgetting."

Collins turned and confronted Drouillard's hawkish gaze. "The Shawnees consort with the British. They will kill an enemy soldier, any who enter their lands north of the Ohio." But he smiled slowly, and the smile softened the sad lines of his face. "I will stay on until Saint Louis, collect my pay, request my discharge, and go with you, Georges Drouillard, to the solitary places that you love."